THE INTROVERT CONFOUNDS INNOCENCE continues the story of the eponymous anti-hero introduced in THE INTROVERT.

With his life disrupted by an unscrupulous work colleague and a bully at his son Toby's school, things go from bad to worse when his neighbor's abusive boyfriend goes missing, plunging the introvert into the center of a murder investigation.

Increasingly hounded by a meddlesome detective, and with his thoughts continually urging him to make people "red and open" and to "achieve it" with his girlfriend Donna, what follows is a sometimes brutal, oftentimes hilarious, and absurdist account of the life of one very anti-social and unexpected anti-hero.

Critical Praise for Michael Paul Michaud

"What a fantastically weird, twisted and absolutely quirky novella *The Introvert* was! So much so, I am not even sure where in the world to begin! The cover is simple, yet eye-catching and pretty much gives you a feel of the wickedly wonderful writing you will stumble across as you delve into the world of *The Introvert*!...Would I recommend this wee novella? You bet your arse I would! I found its originality refreshing, its quirkiness addictive, and the strangeness was absolutely awesome!" ~ Noelle Holton, blogger (CrimeBookJunkie) and author of *Dead Inside*

"Michaud has managed to draw a perfect picture of the main character, which is a character I quickly fell in love with because of his awkwardness and special, yet cute, way of thinking... He just seems like the most adorable and awkward person what so ever. Without spoiling, it kind of scares me that I find a character so adorable when he is able to do the things that the Introvert has done." ~ BOOKNOOKREADING BY MARLIDA

"Similar to that of *American Psycho* with a dash of God Bless America, and yet it was both darker and less violent simultaneously...I really enjoyed reading the story and felt myself laughing or smiling in between the cringes at the main character's internal anger at people and his urges for them to be "red and open." Though the thoughts were gruesome at times, I can't say he was entirely over the top with his reactions. I would love to read more from Michael Paul Michaud, especially if the writing is along the same lines as The Introvert." ~ OnlineBookClub.org

"I simply loved this book…purely entertaining, thought provoking and ultimately beautiful! A perfect weekend read." ~ Halo of Books

"I love how even before the story starts, it says 'For the weirdos,' which made me think, this sounds promising…Oh how I love getting into the minds of weirdos." ~ LittleMissNoSleep

"This is a quirky and quick read about a young man's quest to get through his life without causing too many dramas that upset him. Similar in vein to "The Curious Incident of the Dog in the Night time" where the protagonist is slightly dysfunctional and whose behaviour can be triggered by certain actions by others, leading to unexpected, possibly life changing events. I would recommend it to people who like a bit of black humor, quirky characters and a plot where you are not really sure where you will go." ~ Library Grits (Dianne McKenzie)

"This dark humor novella had readers laughing before it even hit the shelves. Michaud portrays a likable but awkward vacuum salesman who lives an introverted life. Once a past secret comes back to haunt him, he finds himself in the middle of a murder investigation. With lots of wit and charm, The Introvert is sure to please a range of audiences." ~ The Odyssey Online ~ "7 Worthy Books You Might Have Missed From 2016"

ACKNOWLEDGMENTS

I want to thank Andrea Dillon and Andy Thorn for taking the time to read and comment on this story before most people had the opportunity to do so or probably even wanted to, and also to Paul Renwick for F&MFC, and although this isn't much of an acknowledgment section, hopefully they will at least find that they were sufficiently recognized in the circumstances.

THE INTROVERT CONFOUNDS INNOCENCE

MICHAEL PAUL MICHAUD

A Black Opal Books Publication

For the weirdos

THE INTROVERT

CONFOUNDS
INNOCENCE

The Child Psychology Magazine

January ~ Be Sufficiently Happy
February ~ Get Thee To A Huggery!
March ~ Monkey See, Monkey Do
April ~ Good Touch, Bad Touch
May ~ We Are Who We Are
June ~ Bullying Is The New Purple
July ~ Find Your Freud
August ~ Duck, Duck, Goose, Nap
September ~ Blackhawk Down
October ~ Honesty is the Best Policy

CHAPTER 1

A nd what can I get you, young man?"

The gentleman behind the counter was speaking to Toby, who had his face pressed up against the glass, as children are apt to do at ice cream shops.

It wasn't much of an ice cream shop. The line was too long and the glass was terribly smeared and the prices seemed excessive for a simple dairy product, but at least the air conditioning worked well.

The clerk was a thin, older man with a chocolate-smeared apron and a small white cap on his head and a plastic nametag that said "Steve," and I immediatcly figured that this must have been his name because the chances of him wearing the wrong nametag by mistake or perhaps even wearing a fake nametag on purpose as an alias seemed low, and though I didn't completely rule out those possibilities, I settled it in my mind that the gentleman's name was almost certainly Steve.

As Toby hemmed and hawed over what to order, it gave my mind time to think, which seemed to be something that it liked to do, so I wondered what Toby was going to order. Then just as quickly I started wondering why I was wondering what Toby was going to order. Then I started thinking about why I think the way I do and why I'm always wondering about why and how certain things happen, and then I even started wondering if everyone else in the world was like this or if it was just me, and if it was just me, that maybe that made me special, and just as I started wondering about how special I might be, I suddenly shifted to thinking about global warming because it was mid-September and unseasonably warm, and I'd only just thought about the melting icecaps when Toby finally said "Chocolate," pointing as he did.

"A fine decision," said the man who was presumably named Steve.

He was smiling and seemed awfully happy with Toby's decision, and I wondered if he would have reacted the same way had Toby ordered Vanilla, or Pistachio, or Rocky Road, and I also wondered if there was a flavor Toby could have ordered that might have caused him to become despondent, or perhaps even enraged, but then I figured I'd never know for sure unless I stood by the counter and continually watched people order different flavors of ice cream, and though I was somewhat curious about it, I wasn't curious enough to actually do it.

After Steve handed Toby his cone, I paid the cashier and we started for the door. Just then a man walked inside with two young children. One of the children looked vaguely familiar, but then most children looked the same to me so I thought nothing of it, only Toby seemed to startle at seeing that boy, then grew quiet. After they passed we exited through the door and found a table out-side with two chairs and an umbrella where I'd earlier tied up my dog Molly. Toby was still holding his cone and had not yet started licking, which was very unlike most children holding a chocolate ice cream cone, or even most adults for that matter.

"Is anything wrong?" I asked.

Toby didn't answer.

"You will have to eat your ice cream if you don't want it to melt," I said. I said it because it was true.

Toby finally started to lick his ice cream, but I could tell by the way he was eating it that something was both-ering him because he didn't seem to be enjoying it as he normally would, so I figured it must have had something to do with the people who'd just come in.

Toby had recently started pre-school, and the first two weeks had seemingly gone by without incident. By then we had settled into a routine, which was something that I preferred. Donna or I would walk him to school before going to work, and sometimes we'd both walk him if there was time enough before our shifts and it wouldn't get us in trouble with our bosses. Donna would then pick him up from daycare after work and then go home and make dinner, and when I got home, I'd take Molly for a walk. Then we would all have dinner and watch television and then go to bed, and if Donna had had a good day at work and if I hadn't upset her in some fashion, she would usually help me to achieve it, though sometimes she wouldn't help me to achieve it even if she'd had a good day at work and I hadn't upset her in any fashion. I'd read about this being a normal trend in relationships from magazine and newspaper articles, and though I'd initially thought these articles might be joking or exaggerating, it turns out they were actually true.

I watched Toby continue to eat his ice cream slowly and quietly. He finished after five minutes and then I asked him again if anything was wrong. Just then the same man and two boys exited the ice cream shop, and I saw the way that Toby looked over and how his expression changed. The adult was a large, loud man who seemed both strong and flabby at the same time. He was telling a story to the boys and laughing obnoxiously. Once they'd walked away, I again asked Toby what was bothering him.

"Nothing," he said.

"Is that the truth?" I asked.

Toby nodded, but it was a weak nod.

"I see," I said.

I'd started saying "I see" some years ago when I'd heard a police officer say it several times, and soon after I'd incorporated it into my own language. As it turned out, this was a short, easy phrase to say, and it seemed to convey more than just the two words, so it seemed very efficient. I'd sometimes thought about finding that officer to thank him for his contribution to my talking, because I'd read somewhere that imitation is the highest form of flattery, but then I wasn't sure if the officer would feel flattered since he'd been investigating me for two local murders at the time, and maybe he'd even think I was taunting him, so I decided it wouldn't be worth it. I was thinking about all this when Toby started to talk.

"Timmy picks on me."

"I see."

"He's stupid."

I figured that Toby wasn't actually commenting on the boy's intelligence but was just saying this as a child-ish, immature reaction to someone causing him distress. Though I kept open the possibility that Timmy might actually be stupid.

"Which boy was it?" I asked.

Toby didn't answer. By then Molly had come up beside him and he'd started to pet her.

"Was it the red-haired boy?"

He nodded, after a while, still looking down at Molly.

"What has he done?"

"Just stuff."

"What stuff?"

"He pushes me," said Toby.

"What else?"

"He grabs my hair."

He didn't say anything else, so we sat silently for several minutes. Finally, we got up from the table, and I took Molly's leash in one hand and Toby's hand in the other, and we started walking to where I'd parked the car.

For Christmas last year, Donna had given me a subscription to a child psychology magazine to help me better understand children, and though I felt that I understood Toby well enough already, I figured that it couldn't hurt to understand him better starting in January when the first issue arrived, so I wasn't too fussed about it. It also turned out to be helpful in that moment because the June issue had an article called "Bullying Is The New Purple," and even though I didn't understand what the title meant, the article itself was very informative. It said that most bullies were just unhappy people who learned this same behavior from their parents—who were often cowardly, weak-minded people themselves with low self-esteem. There was more to the article than that and a lot more words, but that was the general gist of it. This led me to conclude that Timmy might not only be stupid but also unhappy, and with a cowardly, weak-minded father or mother, and all of this briefly made me feel sorry for

Timmy. Only then I started thinking about the effect this could have on Toby, and I thought back on my own childhood and how some of the boys had been mean to me and picked on me, and I wondered what effect that had had on me and if it had perhaps made me the way that I was. Of course, it was possible I was the way I was already and maybe that was why they chose to pick on me in the first place. This was a paradox—which was to say that it was impossible to determine which came first, like the chicken and the egg.

I thought about discussing "Bullying Is The New Purple" with Toby, but then I figured he was likely too young to understand the nuances of the article, so instead I just told him that bullies were mean people, which seemed to be more or less what the article was saying anyway.

Suddenly, Toby stopped walking.

"I don't want to go to school anymore," he said.

I knelt down to his height and explained that school was a government-regulated activity and that he was statutorily obligated to attend, and though I didn't say it exactly that way because he was four years old, I did say it mostly that way because I wanted my response to be as fair and accurate as possible. Toby just stared at me when I said it, and I thought that maybe he didn't understand what I'd said, but then he started crying, so I concluded that he must have understood it well enough.

He stood defiantly and kept repeating "I don't wanna

go," over and over before I finally took his hand and pulled him along the sidewalk, and I saw people looking over at us as if they were fascinated by this and even Molly had started to bark, and it was apparent that things had soured very quickly since we'd first arrived at the ice cream shop and ordered chocolate ice cream from the man whom I believed was named Steve.

As we approached the car, I saw a man standing in front of it, and, as we got closer I could see that it was a parking attendant. He'd been pressing some buttons on a small black device, and just as we arrived beside the car he walked up to the front of the windshield and placed a ticket beneath one of my wipers.

"We are just ready to leave," I said.

"Meter's expired," is all he said.

I looked at my watch and saw that we were just a couple minutes late.

"Something happened with my son," I said.

The man didn't respond.

"He has been bullied by a child at school," I said.

"Is that right?" said the man. He was already looking at the car parked in front of ours and was again pressing buttons on his device.

I told him that it was indeed true, then asked if he'd read the June issue of *The Child Psychology Magazine*, but he didn't respond to that.

"I would like you to take this ticket back," I said.

My father used to say that you couldn't even spit in

the wind without it costing you money, which was to say that life was expensive and almost anything you did cost money, and the more life went on the more I found this to be true. Things were already tight at home, what with the cost of having a four-year-old and a cat and a dog. I had found Toby in particular to be a significant financial liability, and as the years went on, I felt increasing pressure to sell more vacuums to make up for it. Donna also cost money, but then she also made some money herself, so I figured that part was a wash, even if it actually wasn't.

"Oh would you?" he said.

He laughed when he said it, so it made me wonder if he was mocking me, but then I thought maybe he was just jolly, or perhaps he'd just thought of something funny at that precise moment, so I figured I'd give him the benefit of the doubt.

"I would," I said, and I thought maybe now he would truly consider it.

Instead, the parking attendant shook his head and laughed even louder, and this time I was satisfied that he was indeed laughing at me because I figured the coincidence would have been too great for him to have thought of two funny things both times I'd mentioned the ticket. He then turned around to face me where I was still standing on the sidewalk holding Toby's hand and Molly's leash. Then he told me that my problems weren't his problems and that if I had an issue with it, I could contact the city.

He wasn't much of a parking attendant to be saying these things. Toby was still crying beside me, and Molly had again started to bark, but I could barely hear either one of them because by then my patience had thinned and I was already picturing the parking attendant as red and open.

He still had the smirk on his face, and though I didn't have a weapon on me, I saw a half-brick by the curb, and for a moment I wondered how the brick had ended up that way, and what had happened to the other half, but those thoughts didn't last long because when I looked back up I saw the smirk on the attendant's face, and I figured that as soon as he turned away with his stupid grin and his small black device with the buttons that I could scoop up the half-brick in my hand and move up swiftly behind him and before he could react I'd smash it down into the back of his head, knocking him down instantly and perhaps even rendering him unconscious with that single blow. And then I thought about how I'd nestle down beside him and smash the brick down onto his head over and over and over until his skull caved in and the blood was rushing out from the open wound and how both my hand and the brick would be slick and red and how by then any onlookers would be running away in horror, but then, before I could do any of that, I heard Toby yell "Ouch!"

I looked down and realized that I must have been squeezing his hand so tight that it had caused him pain, so

I immediately let go. The parking attendant was looking curiously in my direction by then so I quickly got Toby and Molly into the car, retrieved the ticket from the windshield, and drove away without saying anything further.

I could see the attendant looking curiously in our direction through the rear view mirror as we drove away, and I immediately felt bad for thinking of him as red and open because I knew that he didn't deserve it, even if he hadn't been very understanding and had perhaps even been mocking me in front of my son.

He might not have been much of a parking attendant, but he certainly didn't deserve it.

CHAPTER 2

There was an article in the March issue of *The Child Psychology Magazine* called "Monkey See, Monkey Do," which immediately appealed to me because I'd always found monkeys to be fascinating creatures, and I also thought it would be a pleasant break from having to learn about people.

As it turned out, the article had nothing to do with monkeys at all, and while this was initially some cause for disappointment, it did end up being a fairly useful article because it talked about how children patterned themselves after parental figures and how they absorbed information at an alarming rate, and how this information shaped their own interactions with people in the years to come. One part of the article dealt with abuse, and it said that children subjected to abuse, even if they only witnessed it, will internalize the violence and that it strongly predisposes them to act out in a similar manner at some unknown future date, which is all a long way of saying that if I had made the parking attendant red and open by bashing his head apart with the half-brick, then this would have predisposed Toby to doing something similar when he grew up.

For the remainder of the drive home I thought about that article and about how fortunate I was to have kept my scary thoughts in my head without letting them escape into the real world where they sometimes went. There were times I hadn't been able to control myself and I couldn't help thinking about how awful it would be if I ever acted on them in front of my son, and though I suppose he could still end up like me regardless, I figured that him seeing me murder another human being with a brick, or even half of a brick, would probably have been a bad start.

We arrived home soon after and I had to carry Toby in from the car because he'd already fallen asleep on the short drive home.

Donna had gone to aerobics, and though she told me they don't call it aerobics anymore and that there were more modern, specialized terms for the classes, I could never remember any of them, so to me she just went to aerobics.

I took Toby upstairs and tucked him into bed for a

nap, which was something children liked to do, and was an important part of their growth cycle according to the August issue of *The Child Psychology Magazine* in an article called "Duck, Duck, Goose, Nap." The article said that naps helped reset neural pathways and repair damaged cells and had other benefits that I couldn't presently remember, but it seemed like it was mostly based in science and I figured the scientists generally knew what they were talking about.

Toby seemed to need naps for all different reasons, and I'd come up with different names for them in my mind, which was to say that I didn't share these names aloud with Donna or anyone else because sometimes the way I thought and said and labeled things made people nervous, since most people didn't think the same way I did. I mostly just kept these sorts of thoughts to myself, and my nap labels were another one of those times.

I figured this was one of Toby's "tantrum naps" because he often got tired after he'd been crying or pitched a fit about one thing or another, and since he'd been crying almost non-stop since I advised him of the government regulations regarding mandatory school attendance, I was satisfied that must have been it, though I did briefly consider that this might be a "trauma nap," which was a nap he'd take after experiencing some upheaval like when his goldfish died, or coming face to face with the boy who'd been bullying him at school as had happened today.

"Will you read me a story, Daddy?" he said, having roused awake.

Toby had recently started asking me to read him stories, even though this was something that his mother liked to do, and something that I liked his mother to do as well.

"Perhaps another time," I said, which was what people generally said when they didn't want to do something and hoped to avoid having to do it by means of postponement until the other party forgot or simply gave up.

"Why?" He whined a little when he said it, which was surely meant to guilt me into conforming.

"I do not believe I would successfully recreate the voices," I said.

Toby looked perplexed by my answer, but the fact was that I had told him the same thing each time he asked. Toby very much enjoyed it when Donna told him stories because she would deploy different voices for the different characters, and I knew that would be difficult for me because it made me feel uncomfortable to speak in any voice that wasn't my own.

"Perhaps Ralph could tell you a story?"

I handed Toby his teddy bear, and although he likely understood there was little chance of Ralph actually telling him a story, he took him all the same, curling his arm tightly around.

After tucking Toby into his bed, I went downstairs with Molly and sat in my favorite green chair and watched some television. It wasn't long after when I heard the front door open.

"Anybody home?"

"Yes," I said, even though she surely already knew this since my car was parked in the driveway.

"So, how was the ice cream?" said Donna, walking into the den. She was still wearing her yellow leotard, even though she didn't actually call it that.

"I didn't have any," I said. "But Toby ordered chocolate."

"Where is he now?"

"He's taking a nap," I said.

"Sugar must have spun him out, eh?"

This was the first time it occurred to me that I may have been mistaken all along about the nap type I'd ascribed and that it might have simply been a "food nap," which was one of the most common type of naps and one enjoyed by adults and children alike, only by then I felt it was too late to go back and re-categorize Toby's nap from a tantrum or trauma nap, so I just committed it to memory and figured to be more careful in the future.

"He was upset," I said. "A boy has been picking on him at school."

"What boy?" she said. Her tone suddenly became very serious, and she came right up in front of me with an angry look on her face, as if maybe I were the person who'd been bullying Toby, rather than just the person delivering the information.

"A boy named Timmy," I said. "We saw him at the ice cream shop. Toby still seemed to enjoy his ice cream, but I don't believe he enjoyed it as much as he normally would have."

Donna didn't care about the ice cream anymore. I knew this because she said, "Who gives a shit about the ice cream?" Then she told me that we had to do something about the boy Timmy.

"What is to be done?" I said.

"We'll speak to the teacher, that's what the hell is going to be done about it." She said it in a loud voice, and again as if I were the person she was angry at. I'd found that Donna was easily governed by her emotions, and that she could become angry or upset very quickly, and it occurred to me that she might even benefit from an occasional tantrum nap.

I'd mentioned something like this to her once before, but for some reason the suggestion had only made her angrier, so I thought better about mentioning it again, so instead all I said was, "I see."

"Yeah, well, we're going to speak to the teacher first thing Monday morning, that's what you're going to see," then she stormed upstairs, presumably to go check on Toby, though I suppose she might have just been going upstairs to remove her leotard that wasn't actually a leotard, and maybe even to take a shower.

Donna came back downstairs an hour later, and it was as if the earlier incident had never occurred because she was back to being her normal self. I was still seated in the green chair and Molly was asleep at my feet.

"Remember that Hayley and Josh are coming over for dinner tonight."

I nodded when she said it, but it was a weak nod. The fact was that I'd been dreading it ever since Donna had told me about the plans last week. Hayley lived next door to us with her dog Mister Muggles. The dog's name apparently came from a fantasy book written by a woman who used to live in her car, only I figured that she probably didn't live in her car anymore if there were people naming their dogs after characters in her books.

It wasn't that I disliked Hayley, but the fact was that I much preferred to be alone and away from people because I already had to endure people all week at work, and I didn't like to talk to people any more than was required. Unfortunately, most people liked to talk an awful lot, even when they had nothing important to say, which I found was most of the time. It had been hard enough to move into a house with Donna after she became pregnant, and then when Toby arrived there were three of us, not to mention Molly and the cat, and Bob the turtle whose death last year had contributed to Toby's first trauma nap.

Donna was making orange chicken, and they would be coming over whether I liked it or not, so I figured there was no sense belaboring the point in my mind. Instead I just started thinking about the half-brick again, wondering what happened to the second half, and even felt a bit sorry for it being broken apart and separated from its other half, and maybe even from the rest of its brick family and whatever wall it was supposed to be a part of, though I did recognize this to be somewhat absurd, so I didn't feel very sorry for the half-brick for very long.

CHAPTER 3

They arrived promptly at seven.

Hayley handed Donna a bottle of wine and a small gift bag, then they hugged, which was something people increasingly liked to do, and even though I'd stood back purposely and made my body rigid, she still approached me for a hug, so there was no way to avoid it.

"Where's Mister Muggles?" I asked, after she'd finally released me.

Mister Muggles was her golden retriever, and though I thought that was an odd name to give a pet, he was a beautiful dog, and I could tell that he was happy and well cared for, and that was really all that mattered.

"Oh, I think he can make it on his own for a few hours," she said, smiling.

"I see," only by then I wasn't thinking so much about Mister Muggles as I was wondering if they were really going to be here that long, and though I hoped she was just speaking loosely or perhaps was overestimating the time, I figured there was little that could be done about it at that point.

By then, Molly had run in amongst us.

"And how's my Mollydog?" said Hayley, kneeling down to greet her. She liked to call Molly by an extended version of her name that included adding her species at the end, and though I never called her anything but "Molly," the longer name didn't seem to bother her and I think maybe she even liked it because of the way she was gyrating and trying to lick Hayley's face.

That's when her boyfriend Josh reached out and we shook hands. It was a long, hard handshake, and it seemed as if he didn't want to let go first, so finally I let go.

Hayley had been our neighbor ever since we'd moved here nearly four years ago, and in many ways she reminded me of Donna when I first knew her because she seemed to always be dating different men and generally was dissatisfied with all of them for one reason or another. From what I'd gathered from Donna, Hayley had been seeing Josh for several months now, and though she was happy in some ways, she wasn't all the way happy. It seemed that Josh liked to drink and that once he'd even grabbed her forcefully by the arm and left a bruise. Donna hadn't actually seen it, but some women in the neighborhood had gossiped about it as women sometimes do.

This reminded me of the January issue of *The Child Psychology Magazine* because there was an article inside called "Be Sufficiently Happy" written by a child psychologist, and it said that modern parents had unrealistic expectations of how happy their children should be, and this in turn created impossible expectations of happiness in the children, later leading to anxiety, depression, and feelings of general dissatisfaction with life. The article said that pure happiness was a myth and shouldn't be pursued, and that we should just aim to ensure that our children were *sufficiently* happy, and that if they were mostly happy then that should be good enough, and there was no benefit to dwelling on small amounts of unhappiness. According to the psychologist, if you were sufficiently happy then you should just call yourself happy, and I couldn't help thinking that Hayley must have at least been sufficiently happy with Josh.

This was only the second time I'd met him. The first had been at a BBQ this summer, and I remember Josh being very loud and trying hard to make friends with everyone. I also remember how he talked to Hayley and how he was rather rude and bossy, and I remember wondering why she would want to spend her time with someone like that, but then I figured that was her choice so I wasn't too fussed about it.

I'd found through life that the louder the person was,

the quieter I'd become, and I remember spending much of that BBQ standing with Molly by the back fence and watching Toby play with some of the other kids, only now Toby was upstairs playing with his toys, Molly had gone off somewhere to sleep, and there wasn't even a fence to stand by.

Donna led us into the living room where we all sat down. She poured some wine for Hayley while Josh and I had beer and then Donna opened the gift that Hayley had brought, and it turned out to be a small ceramic cow.

"It's a milk dispenser," said Hayley.

"Oh, how sweet," said Donna. "I've seen this before. The McGibbons have one!"

"That's where I first saw it too. They're all the rage," said Hayley. "I even bought one for myself."

The girls laughed while neither myself or Josh made a sound.

"Isn't this great, honey?"

Donna liked to call me "Honey" when she was feeling playful and affectionate, and this was apparently one of those times. Then she handed me the ceramic cow, and I looked at it for a few moments and nodded to be polite. Then we all engaged in small talk for about half an hour which was a small form of torture to me, and I was much relieved when we finally moved to the dining room table for dinner because then at least I could fill my mouth with food and have a justifiable reason not to talk.

As we ate our dinner, Donna asked Josh about his

work and he said "Roofing," which I understood to be a euphemism for unemployment.

"Sounds interesting," said Donna. "Is it hard work?"

"Depends on the season," he said, but then he didn't elaborate.

I'd found that some people didn't elaborate because they just didn't have much to say or had trouble articulating themselves in a meaningful way. But others didn't elaborate because they didn't have a good answer or it was an uncomfortable topic, so they would answer with a vague, ambiguous statement and hope the matter would go away. This was called "diffusing discomfort" and was actually a strategy I learned from my employer, who taught us to always diffuse customer discomfort by interjecting ambiguous or generalized statements into the conversation as necessary. Given how loud Josh usually was, I figured that his employment must have been an uncomfortable topic for him based on how he'd suddenly become very quiet.

"I sell vacuums," I said.

This was my first unprompted contribution to the conversation, and I was hoping that it might satisfy them for a while, but then Hayley started asking me questions.

"How is it that you get people to buy so many vacuums?" she asked. "Donna says you're one of the best salesmen she's ever seen."

This last part was probably true, but I also think Donna probably hadn't known many other salespeople in her life, so I wondered if much weight should be given to her opinion. Donna and I worked for the same company, and though we used to work together in the same location, she'd accepted a position at another office to avoid the appearance of partiality. The company seemed to believe that Donna might show me preferential treatment and send extra customers my way. I'd thought this was unlikely, until she actually started to do it. In this way, I felt her transfer was appropriate. I think it also helped our relationship to have some time apart, even if I didn't mention this last part to Donna.

"Everyone needs to buy a vacuum," I responded.

"I suppose so," said Hayley. "But don't most people already have a vacuum cleaner at home?"

"Most do," I said. "But they are usually old or unsafe or unreliable, and who wants a vacuum like that?" I said.

Nobody seemed to have an answer for this, so the subject was soon dropped, which suited me fine, as I wasn't really looking for an answer to the question.

Donna served salad after dinner because she'd read somewhere that this was how they did it in Europe, and even if we didn't have a lot of money and couldn't travel to Paris or Rome or Vienna and live like those people, then I suppose she figured that we could at least eat like them.

She brought out the salad and placed it in front of everyone, and Josh remarked "That's a lot of kale," and then both Donna and Hayley started to laugh, presumably because it was a kale salad and his observation was an obvious one. However, I didn't laugh because I found his comment entirely appropriate and accurate, and it even sounded like something I might say. Josh also didn't laugh, and in fact his face turned sour, and he even seemed angry.

That's when I said, "It *is* a lot of kale," and both Donna and Hayley laughed again even louder, and then even Josh started to laugh, even though my comment wasn't meant to be funny at all but was just meant to concur with what Josh had just said.

They continued to talk and I contributed as necessary and soon dinner was over and I accompanied Josh to the front porch because he wanted to smoke a cigar.

"You want one?" he said, pulling a second out of his coat pocket.

"No, thank you."

He just shrugged and tucked the second cigar back into his pocket. A moment later, he was puffing it where we stood and the wind carried some of it back toward me and it made me cough, but he didn't move, so I did. By then, he was on at least his fifth beer of the night and I could tell he was impaired by his slow movements and slurred speech.

"Nice area you got here," he said.

"Yes," I said. And he was right. Our house was right at the corner of a quiet suburban intersection, and there was a big field with a park kitty-corner to where we were standing and where the kids and the dogs could run and play. It was a nice neighborhood, and we likely could not have afforded to buy here if Donna's parents hadn't loaned us some money for the down payment.

"You been with your lady long?" he said, taking a long sip from his bottle.

"I have been seeing Donna for almost five years," I said, then a look came on his face very similar to the parking attendant's when I'd asked him to take back the ticket.

"Isn't your kid four?"

"Yes."

"So, shotgun wedding, eh?"

"No," I said.

"Yeah, you bet your ass," he said, then hit me on my arm. It wasn't an angry punch, but more like a playful punch that men sometimes did.

"We aren't married," I said. I said it because it was true, but also because I didn't want him to continue with his misapprehension.

"Yeah, well, marriage isn't what it used to be anyway."

I wasn't exactly sure what he meant by that, so I said "I suppose," in order to continue with the conversation. "Do you plan to wed Hayley?" I asked, since we'd just been discussing marriage.

Only the question seemed to disturb him because he drew back a step with a shocked look in his face and said,

"Jesus, you fucking serious?" and though I wasn't sure if it was an actual question rather than a rhetorical question, I decided to answer it anyway.

"Yes," I said.

He seemed to settle down a bit and leaned up against one of the brick pillars.

"Marriage is a one-way ticket to misery town, and there ain't no refund," he said.

I figured that this was probably a metaphor, and though I didn't know precisely what he meant by it, I could at least tell that he didn't think highly of marriage.

"I see," I said, then added, "Do you suppose that Hayley feels the same?"

"How the hell can I know with women? One thing's for sure, whatever she may believe about marriage, she sure as hell believes in busting my balls."

I didn't respond to that because I wasn't sure how. Then he went on and said, "Maybe if she treated me half as good as she does that fucking mutt..." and then he took another swig from his beer.

"I don't believe Mister Muggles is a mutt. I believe that he is a pure breed."

Josh looked at me queerly when I said it. That's when I saw the Morrison kid run by us on the sidewalk. He had a cape and helmet on even though it wasn't Halloween for another six weeks. He turned and waved at us, and I waved back. Then so did Josh, only he did so by raising up his beer as if in a toast.

"What in the hell was that?" he said after the Morrison boy had moved on up the sidewalk.

"He lives a few houses down," I said.

"Yeah, I think I've seen him around. What's his story, anyway?"

"I believe that he goes to a special school," I said.

"Parents sniffed a lot of glue, eh?"

I didn't respond.

"Yeah, well I guess every neighborhood needs a retard kid." Then he took another long sip of his beer.

Whereas the first time I'd met Josh, I'd simply found him to be loud and obnoxious, I now concluded that he wasn't a very good person, and though previously I'd just wanted to remove myself from the conversation, this was the first time I started thinking some of my scary thoughts about him.

Just then Hayley and Donna came out onto the porch.

"We thought we'd lost you," said Hayley, cozying up beside Josh, and hooking her arm under his.

She was clearly joking, only I wasn't in the mood for jokes, and I could see that Josh felt the same way because he didn't smile and instead just took another sip of his beer and polished off the bottle.

"It's getting late," she said. "I think we better get going."

"I think we got time for one more," said Josh.

"I think you've had just about enough," she said, and

I saw how his face bent nasty when she said it.

The conversation petered out abruptly at that point, and there seemed a sudden heaviness in the air. After a short period of silence, everyone said their goodbyes, and Hayley and Josh walked away quietly before disappearing from sight.

I didn't disclose to Donna what he'd been saying or how he'd been acting, and though I didn't much want him coming back here, I figured this was a conversation that could be held for later, in the event that Donna ever wished to invite them over again.

My father used to tell me "Don't borrow trouble," which meant that with enough real troubles in the world, there was no sense engaging any additional trouble until it actually presented itself, so I decided not to borrow any trouble that night.

CHAPTER 4

O n Monday, Donna and I arrived early at Toby's pre-school so we could talk to his teacher. Toby went along with us quite willingly, which meant he'd either not meant what he'd said on Saturday about never returning to school, or else he'd resigned himself to the necessity of his attendance and had taken the last two days to find peace with this reality. Either that or he'd just forgotten.

Toby's teacher was a young woman named Miss Mullen. We had Toby sit on the classroom floor with some toys and then Miss Mullen joined us out in the hallway where Donna told her about the bullying at the hand of Timmy.

"Thank you for bringing this to our attention," she

said. "I'll pay close attention to them from now on."

"Have you seen any of it?" asked Donna.

Miss Mullen shook her head. "To be honest, kids are always picking at each other in one way or another, but then they usually forget about it ten seconds later. I hadn't noticed anything particular between Toby and Timmy."

"Toby did not wish to return to school," I said.

"Yes, I can imagine."

"I advised him that school was a government-regulated activity and that he was required to attend."

She didn't say anything to this, but had a look on her face as if she might be confused, so I went back over what I'd just said in my mind, only to me it didn't seem very complicated, so then I figured that maybe she was just easily confused.

"We just wanted to make sure you'll keep a careful watch on the situation," said Donna.

"Of course," she responded.

After that, we went back inside to say goodbye to Toby, then left before any of the other kids arrived, and I was happy that the matter had been put to rest.

ುು

I drove straight to work after that and even arrived fifteen minutes early, which always made my boss happy. I then proceeded to sell five vacuum cleaners, which was a decent haul in one day since I worked on commission.

I was preparing to leave at the end of the day when my boss stopped by my cubicle.

"Well, hello there," he said.

His name was Mr. Peters and he'd been my boss for the last six years, which was an awful long time for management in a retail organization because they were always getting promoted or relocated or fired for pilfering, though I supposed there could be other reasons they could be fired, like just being a bad boss. Given that Mr. Peters had been there for longer than any of my former bosses, I concluded that he at least wasn't pilfering, though I just as quickly took that conclusion back in my mind because I recognized the possibility that perhaps he was indeed pilfering but just hadn't been caught yet.

I noticed that Mr. Peters was staring at me, and I realized that I hadn't responded to him yet, so I said "Hello," and then turned to gather my lunch bag.

"I wanted to let you know that we have a new salesman starting tomorrow. Just hired him today."

I didn't comment because I'd found that with most people it was best to talk as little as absolutely possible because many people were sensitive and easily offended and so you might say the wrong thing or perhaps offend them in some way that you hadn't imagined, and I felt this was particularly true when it came to bosses. In my view, life goes easier the less you speak. I also figured that personnel decisions were none of my business, and that if he wanted my input he'd probably come right out and ask, though I hoped he wouldn't.

"I thought we might put him right here," he said, slamming his palm down on the empty desk beside mine that had been vacated last month when the last employee up and quit in the middle of the day. I hadn't found it to be much of a surprise that he quit because he once told me that if he were still working here in five years that I had permission to shoot him in the head, and though I figured he was likely just exaggerating when he said that, there remains the possibility that he wasn't, and that his quitting was an act of self-preservation.

I thought maybe that was all that Mr. Peters wanted to say, so I nodded at him and started to walk away when all of a sudden he called out, "Whoa, easy there, tiger," and then he placed his hand on my shoulder, and though I generally disliked it when people put their hands on me without my consent, I figured he didn't mean anything by it, and it certainly didn't rise to some of the stuff they talked about in the April issue of *The Child Psychology Magazine* in an article called "Good Touch, Bad Touch," which focused mostly on how some adults liked to achieve it with children.

I turned around to face him and saw that Mr. Peters had a smile on his face, and that's when he told me that the new employee's name was Gordon and that he'd already been through some training at head office but that I should help him out here and there as needed. Then he added that Gordon was blind, but that's what made him perfect for selling vacuums over the phone because nobody would judge him or discriminate against him and that he hoped that neither would I.

"I see," I said.

"He comes highly recommended." Mr. Peters went on to tell me that Gordon used to work for a large electronics chain that had recently gone out of business. I knew the one that he was talking about because it was all over the news because the employees showed up for work one Saturday morning to find all the doors locked. I'd once bought a television from that chain, only I returned it because I didn't much like the remote control. In hindsight it was probably more trouble than it was worth to return a television simply because the remote control wasn't convenient, but then I figured that other people likely returned products for even less reason than that. "He was their lead appliance salesman for ten years straight," said Peters.

While this was surely good news for the company, it also seemed that Gordon would present competition for some of our monthly contests. In addition to earning commission, the company sometimes ran contests where we could earn extra money or prizes, and I was usually in contention for most of the contests since I consistently sold a lot of vacuums. Based on what Mr. Peters had just told me about Gordon, I immediately felt threatened by him, which seemed unfair since he was blind and recently unemployed. I also wondered if it would have made any difference to Gordon's employment if I hadn't returned the television two years ago, only then I figured that the possibility was remote. Then I realized that I'd just used the term "remote" in my mind and thought that was a humorous coincidence to have selected that word, so I started to laugh.

"Something funny?" asked Mr. Peters.

"No," I said, because I wasn't confident I could explain it to him. He just looked at me curiously and finally said, "Anyway, he'll be in tomorrow. If you could help him out I'd really appreciate it."

"Of course," I said, only I was already thinking it might be better if I didn't help him very much or if I might even sabotage him in a moment of weakness. Only then I felt ashamed for even thinking it, since he was blind and recently unemployed, and since I may have contributed in some small way to his unemployment, even if this possibility was remote.

CHAPTER 5

I arrived home a few minutes late because of my chat with Mr. Peters.

I stepped out of my car and was immediately approached from the side by Mister Muggles. He put his wet nose up to my hand and I petted him on his head and said "Who's a good boy" even though he couldn't actually speak English and there was no hope he'd answer. That's when I looked up and I saw Hayley on her front porch, so I waved. I wondered if she saw me because she had on a pair of dark-rimmed sunglasses, only then she waved back so I wasn't wondering for very long. Then she called for Mr. Muggles, and he went running up to the door, and they immediately went inside. I found it odd that she hadn't waited to say hello, but then I figured she probably had her reasons so I wasn't too fussed about it.

I went inside and Molly met me at the door, and she was wagging her tail and carrying on as she always did. Usually, Toby would also come running to meet me and yell "Daddy" and carry on similarly to Molly, but today he didn't come. We also had a cat named Whiskers, and though it was a rather trite name for a cat, we'd allowed Toby to name him and that was the name he picked, so there wasn't much to be done about it. Unlike Molly and Toby, Whiskers rarely greeted me at the door, and this was just another one of those times that he didn't.

Molly trailed me into the kitchen where I put away my lunch bag and that's when I saw Donna chopping some carrots, and it appeared that she was crying, and though I should probably have been more concerned with what it was that had upset her, the first though that entered my mind was actually about the carrots and whether they were meant for a salad or some sort of stir fry, or maybe even something else I hadn't even thought of.

"Is something wrong?" I asked.

Donna didn't answer at first and instead just kept chopping the carrots. I used to just walk away when this would happen, assuming that Donna wasn't in the mood to talk, but then every time I did she would almost immediately start talking and perhaps even be offended that I'd walked away. As time went on, I'd learned to just wait there silently and more often than not she would just start talking on her own, and soon enough she did.

"I picked up Toby from daycare," she said.

It seemed like there was likely more to the story because she always picked up Toby from daycare and this was the first time I could remember that she'd been crying and chopping carrots after doing so. I waited again for her to speak, and this gave me sufficient time to look around, and I soon saw a large bowl with some lettuce and tomatoes and onions and concluded that the carrots must indeed be for a salad, so I was at least relieved that that mystery had been put to rest.

"He got in a fight," she said finally, resting the knife down at her side. Then she stiffened up and said that it was that Timmy kid again, and that Toby had apparently confronted him about pulling his hair, and then Timmy had punched Toby in the eye. "I called the school as soon as I got home and left a message for Miss Mullen to contact us." By then her mood had shifted from sad to angry.

"How is Toby?" I asked.

"He's upstairs asleep."

"I see."

I figured this was likely one of his trauma naps, and although he sometimes slept through those fairly well, I figured I should at least check in on him and perhaps even have a man to man chat with him if he were interested, and which was something most of the dads did on the television shows I watched and that my own father sometimes did with me unless he left it to the counselors.

I told Donna that I'd go see him, and so I went upstairs and crept slowly into his room, and as soon as I did he opened his eyes, one of which I could see was swollen.

"Daddy?" he said.

"Yes."

I sat on the bed, but he didn't say anything further, and I could see in his face that he'd been crying. I wondered what I should say, and then I thought of February's issue of *The Child Psychology Magazine* because there was an article in it called "Get Thee To A Huggery!" and though I thought it might be an article about Valentine's Day given the title and the month, it was actually an article about how human beings benefit from hugs for their growth and their mental health, and how this was especially true when it came to children. Just like naps, hugs had apparently been scientifically proven to help children with depression, stress, and anxiety, and I felt in that moment there was a good chance Toby might be suffering from all three.

The name of the article apparently came from *Hamlet*, which was a play by William Shakespeare about a man who set out for revenge against his father's killer, but how he mostly just descended into madness and spoke to people who weren't really there, and though I don't remember the specific line in the play, I thought that more hugs and naps might have helped Hamlet, and I figured they might even have helped Macbeth.

I leaned over and hugged Toby, and he hugged me back, and this seemed to settle him. Then he sat up in his bed and rubbed his eyes with both hands.

"Your mother told me that you were struck by Timmy."

Toby nodded.

"And that Timmy pulled your hair?"

Again he nodded.

"We will speak with your teacher tomorrow," I said.

Still Toby didn't say anything, so we just sat there in silence and then I finally tucked him back in bed and went to our bedroom to shower and change, and I was thinking about how awful bullying was and how it might have a negative effect on my child. I was also thinking by then, after giving the matter more thought, that the naps probably wouldn't have helped Macbeth after all, since he'd been rather badly manipulated by Lady Macbeth, and so there wasn't much that could be done about that.

By the time I'd showered and changed, Donna was putting dinner on the table and Toby was up and about. When we sat down to eat, I could see that Donna was still upset, only she was putting on a brave face for our son.

I watched as Toby ate his meatloaf with his black eye, and it was only after a moment that I realized I'd been squeezing my utensil so tightly that the ends of my fingers had started to turn white, so I loosened my grip on the knife and allowed the blood to go back to where it belonged, and that's when I noticed Donna staring at me from across the table. I resumed eating my dinner and tried not to think about it, but the more I tried to push them away the more powerful the thoughts became, so finally I just let the thoughts wash over me, and soon enough I started to feel better, eating the meatloaf with my family, and quietly thinking of young Timmy as red and open.

CHAPTER 6

I arrived at work the next morning fifteen minutes early, which was something I always tried to do, and something that kept the bosses happy.

As I approached my workstation I saw a small black man seated beside my desk, and I wondered where he came from and why he was sitting there, only in the next moment I realized that this must be Gordon. Then I thought about how people have preconceived notions and how I'd immediately identified the name Gordon with a white person, and I wondered why my mind did that when Gordon could just as easily have been black, or Asian, or who knows what else. I was also thinking about why Mr. Peters hadn't mentioned that Gordon was black, only then I thought that maybe it would have been racist if he'd done so, and even if it wouldn't have been full-on racist like the KKK or the Nazis, that if he'd made an issue about Gordon's skin color then it still could have been considered sufficiently racist. Also, although Gordon's skin color was darker than mine, it wasn't all the way dark, so that may have been another reason Mr. Peters didn't mention it.

"Hello?"

"Hello," I said.

"I'm Gordon," he said, extending his hand in my general direction. He was wearing dark glasses like Hayley had been wearing, so I couldn't see which way his eyes were looking.

"I understand that you are blind," I said.

He drew his hand back when I said this.

"Legally blind," he responded.

"I see," I said, and then I laughed out loud because I realized that I'd just said "I see" in a conversation about blindness. Gordon didn't laugh when I said this, so I explained it to him, only he still didn't laugh.

"Yeah," he said hesitantly, "well, Frank said maybe you could show me the company database?"

Frank was Mr. Peters, only I never called him Frank because my parents had always told me to address authority by mister or missus and I never forgot that. There were other things they tried to teach me that didn't always stick due to what my counselors called "poor impulse control," but since I'd never had any impulse to call

Mr. Peters by his first name, this was one of their lessons that was easy to follow, and so I did.

"You still there?" said Gordon.

"Yes," I said, and I was just about to answer him when I noticed the phone on his desk. It was a special phone with a braille keypad, and I couldn't help but think about how far technology had come since I was a child, and how blind people probably would have been rendered doing simple, menial tasks back then, and now here was Gordon who was both blind and black and could apparently accomplish anything anyone else could, and I felt that reflected well on him.

"You still there?" he asked.

"Yes," I said. Then I saw him shake his head a little bit, and I could tell that he was frustrated or annoyed with me for some reason based on his body language.

"So, about that database?" he said.

The company kept a database of names and contact information of previous customers. If it had been more than a year since their last purchase then anyone was allowed to contact them, but if it had been a year or less then only the salesperson who sold them their last vacuum was allowed to contact them. This was meant to reward the salesperson and to encourage loyalty with our customers. There was also a list of potential customers that the company had acquired from various databanks, and this was what we worked from most of the time. I explained to Gordon where the database was saved and was preparing to show him when I saw him type a few things into his keyboard and all of a sudden the list came up onto his screen.

"So you can see, after all?" I said.

"Not very well, but I have these to tell me what's on the screen." Gordon motioned to his earphones, and while I had originally thought that maybe he just had those to listen to music, it turns out that he'd installed a special program into his computer that helped him navigate through its contents. He also had a special braille keyboard and I could see that he was already typing information into some sort of spreadsheet. I started thinking that in many ways Gordon was like a bat because he was able to rely on his other senses and get the job done just as well as the rest of us. I was thinking this about the bat, and then I decided to share it with him because I thought he might be interested in the comparison, but instead he just stared back at me with a funny look in his face.

"A bat?" he asked, turning in my direction. "You fucking serious?"

"Yes," I said.

"That because I'm black?"

"No," I said.

Then I saw him shake his head for the second time and he started clicking a few things on his keyboard and then he picked up the phone and made a call. The next thing I heard he was on the phone with someone named Mrs. Bennett, and I could hear him talking about the benefits of our new, healthy, vacuum technology which he must have learned at orientation, and he was on the phone for an awfully long time and he was even laughing and talking about Europe, which had no connection to vacuums at all, and soon after that I heard him taking down her order.

"Congratulations," I said, after he'd hung up the phone.

"Thanks."

"If you sell vacuums that easily, then you will surely make the bosses happy, and that usually makes for easier days at work."

"Oh, it does, does it?"

"Yes," I said. "Also, we run contests sometimes and you may be able to earn extra money or prizes if you win one of the contests."

"Thanks," he said, only he was still looking at me strangely, so I tried to think about some of the things I'd said and if anything was odd, but nothing came to mind.

Only then I started thinking about the bat comment, and it occurred to me in that moment that most bats are black, or at least that's how they're depicted in cartoons and on Halloween decorations, so I thought that maybe somehow this had offended him, even though I hadn't actually considered the color of his skin at all, but I was thinking about how bats have heightened sensory perception which allows them to hone in on bugs for food and to fly quickly around stalagmites and other obstacles, and I

figured that if bats could do that with bugs and stalagmites that maybe Gordon could do the same sort of thing
with special phones and keypads. Then I thought about
the January issue of *The Child Psychology Magazine*
about being sufficiently happy, and I thought that maybe
he wasn't even sufficiently black to consider himself
black, and that perhaps that was why he was offended. I
was thinking of all of this in my mind and then I said it,
hoping Gordon might better understand my earlier bat
comment. Instead he just looked at me in the same way
that he'd done before.

"Sufficiently black?" he said.

"Yes," I said.

Still he just stared at me. "You fucking with me?"

"No," I said.

He stared at me for a while longer. "You eat a lot of
paste as a kid?"

"No," I said.

"You sure?"

"Yes," I said.

After this we didn't speak anymore, and Gordon
went back to pushing buttons on his specially designed
devices.

I had often found it difficult communicating with my
colleagues, and this seemed to be another one of those
times.

And while I thought that it might be different with
Gordon, it turns out that people are all very much the

same, even those who are sufficiently blind and sufficiently black.

CHAPTER 7

The next afternoon we went to Toby's school where we sat down with the principal and Timmy's parents. Miss Mullen was also there, but she remained standing, so although we sat down with the rest, I suppose we didn't actually sit down with Miss Mullen.

Timmy's father was indeed the same flabby-strong man I'd seen at the ice cream shop last weekend, where Toby had ordered the chocolate cone from the man who I figured was named Steve.

His wife was much smaller than he was and seemed very quiet and meek, and maybe even quieter than me. We'd arrived at the school at virtually the same time and I saw that their truck had a bumper sticker with the confederate flag on it. This was the flag used by the South in the Civil War. The Civil War was fought over some white people thinking they were better than black people and also their desire to keep their labor costs down, and I couldn't help think that if the South had won the war, it's possible that Gordon would now be working in our office for free, and he probably wouldn't even qualify for any of the contests.

"I want to thank you all for coming today," said the principal, drawing my attention.

He wasn't much of a principal. He was a large, balding man and his nose was too big for his face. He also spoke to us in the same slow, measured tone that he probably used on the children.

"In cases such as this, once a concern has been raised, we feel it's important to bring the parents together to discuss the best way to approach this opportunity."

"Opportunity?" said Timmy's father.

I'd learned at my company that the word opportunity was a corporate euphemism for the word problem. They'd taught us that upset customers weren't actually a bad thing since it presented an opportunity to demonstrate how well we could problem solve, or it gave us an opportunity to work on our patience, or to upgrade the customer to a better product and make extra money. According to my company, there were no problems but only opportunities, and it seemed as if the principal had adopted the same philosophy.

"You see," said the principal, "I often find that this is just the kids' way of telling us that something isn't right, and this is our opportunity to discover what the issue is and to correct it."

This was the second time he'd used the word opportunity, and I couldn't help but wonder if perhaps he'd sold vacuums before becoming a principal, but I didn't wonder it strongly enough to ask him. I was also thinking about the time that one of our customers came in to complain about his order and how he was berating the secretary and how my boss later told us that this was just an opportunity to show compassion and understanding and to help make things right and to ensure that we would have a customer for life. Unfortunately, this same customer returned a few weeks later, and it turned out to be just an opportunity to phone the police and have him arrested for assault and battery. Our bosses never mentioned him again after that, and I think maybe even they would have admitted that the incident wasn't as much an opportunity as it was a genuine problem.

"It's really a good thing," said the principal, "when you think of it that way."

"A good thing?" said Donna.

"Yes, well, you see, the issue between Toby and Timothy might simply be a manifestation of some frustration, or perhaps an attention-seeking device that is in no way personal to one another."

I could see that Timmy's father didn't see this so

much as an opportunity as much as a tremendous inconvenience because he was looking rather stone-faced at the principal, and I could see his cheeks were getting red.

"Can't kids just be kids without calling the National Guard?" said Timmy's father, leaning forward as he did

It was clear that he didn't think much of any of this, only then Donna turned sharply toward him and said "Easy to say when it's not your kid getting picked on," and I could see that he didn't much like what was said, or maybe who said it, because he bristled in his seat and I think maybe his cheeks went even redder.

"I understand your frustration, both of you. But trust me when I say that these incidents are common with children. Most of the time it all blows over within a matter of weeks, if not days."

Both Donna and Timmy's father then settled back into their seats, even though it appeared as if both of them still wanted to speak.

"What we normally do is give the kids a timeout," said Miss Mullen. She was smiling widely as she said it, and as if all of this was very pleasant. "However, this case may require additional intervention."

"Additional intervention is when we institute an action plan," said the principal.

"Action plan?" said Donna.

"Yes. We've found great success with our action plans. They were quite a discovery," he added.

"Columbus find them?" said Timmy's father.

I looked up when he said this and saw that Miss Mullen was still smiling as widely as before, and possibly even wider, only it was one of those exaggerated smiles that people sometimes have when they don't want to smile at all, but just don't know what else to do.

"And what would this involve, exactly?"

This was the first time I'd heard Timmy's mother speak, and it seemed as if something about it bothered her husband, because he sneered when she said it, and even shook his head back and forth.

"It could be a variety of things," said the principal, only by then his friendly tone was waning. "Sometimes it simply involves more quiet time. Other times we place the students together so they can learn to appreciate and embrace their differences."

"These are four-year-olds," said Timmy's father.

"Yes, most are four," said the principal.

"And we're talking about action plans?"

"They have been found to be valuable instruments," the principal said.

I saw Timmy's father roll his eyes.

"In the meantime," said the principal, "if you could both speak to your children about bullying. Studies have shown that parents have an incalculable effect on children's interpersonal relationships."

"Incalculable?" said Timmy's father.

The principal nodded.

"Then how do you calculate it?" he said, which I thought was a fair point.

The principal didn't say anything after this, and then suddenly Timmy's father stood up and said that he wanted to go outside for some fresh air and then immediately stepped out of the room. When I looked back up I saw the principal and Miss Mullen staring back at me, and then I looked over and even Donna was staring at me, so I figured that maybe this was a sign that I was supposed to get up and go outside too, so I got up and I did.

I found Timmy's father standing by the front steps with a cigarette in his mouth. He was smiling and shaking his head as I approached.

"You believe this shit?"

I stepped up beside him but didn't say anything. Then he took a long drag on his cigarette and blew it into the wind, only some of it came back into my face.

"Musta quit these ten times," he said, which to me didn't seem accurate, since if he'd actually quit smoking then he only would have quit once, whereas in reality he had only attempted to quit ten times and failed each time. I felt that at best he could claim that he'd temporarily postponed his smoking over the course of ten intervals, and though I'd shared this thought with other smokers in the past, it had usually not been well received, so I decided not to mention it.

"Perhaps we could try the principal's suggestions," I said.

"You think so, eh?"

"It seems that they have some experience in these matters."

He let out another big puff of smoke into the air, and again some of it came back into my face with the wind, but just like Josh with the cigar, he didn't seem to care.

"Bunch of bureaucratic liberal bullshit. Boys fight at school. Hell, I got my ass kicked good a few times. It made a man out of me."

"I do not wish to see Toby harmed."

He turned and looked at me in much the same way he'd looked at the principal when he'd mentioned the action plans. Then he blew out another breath of smoke, and again I started to cough. He apologized after I was done, but he also had a smirk on his face, so it didn't seem very sincere. Then he leaned forward against a railing and got a serious look in his face.

"You know, they're going to turn our kids into a couple of faggots."

Timmy's father reminded me an awful lot of Josh, which was to say that he was rude and I didn't much like him. I also didn't understand how the principal's action plans were likely to turn either of our sons into homosexuals. My parents had taught me that people generally came out the way they did, and that included whether they were tall or short or smart or stupid or gay or straight. I'd read the same thing in the May issue of *The Child Psychology Magazine* in an article called "We Are

Who We Are." The article suggested that people were generally coded the way they were from birth, and that things like height and skin color and sexual orientation were fairly well determined from the moment of conception. The article was meant to encourage parents to accept their children for who they were and who they grew up to be, since most people couldn't help acting or feeling the way that they did. I figured that Timmy's father hadn't read the article based on what he'd just said, so I told him about it and asked him if he might like to borrow my copy, only he turned and looked at me funny when I did.

"You're kidding, right?"

"No," I said, and again he shook his head.

"Look, kids have to be kids. So they fight. Scrape a knee now and again."

"Toby is upset by it."

"Can't wrap 'em in bubble wrap."

"He does not wish to attend school anymore."

Timmy's father turned to face me. The look on his face had changed to become more hostile. "And you're putting that on my boy?"

"It would seem that Timmy has taken an interest in taunting Toby."

"An interest?"

"Yes."

"And Toby is upset by it, that right?"

"That is correct."

I thought that perhaps we were making some positive

headway, only then Timmy's father leaned in real close, and I could smell his rancid breath with the cigarette smoke, and he wrapped his large flabby-strong arm around my shoulders and whispered into my ear, "Look, you don't want your son turning into a pussy, do you?" And then he let go of me and leaned back down against the railing and went back to his smoking, and that's when I felt the blood swelling up in my throat, and in that moment more than anything I wanted to see Timmy's father red and open.

I quickly looked around and saw that we were alone, so I reached into my pocket and took out my Swiss Army knife with the polar bear on the handle and carefully opened it up to the large knife and then I stabbed down with all my might into the back of his neck, and when he turned around I could see his eyes were wide in fear and surprise and that's when I jammed the blade directly into his jugular and jerked the blade down opening a three inch-gash. He immediately collapsed to the ground with his hands overtop of the wound, but by then it was too late and he squirmed helplessly on the ground where he flailed and gurgled and I watched as red bubbles started forming at his lips and how the bubbles eventually popped as his face went still and his eyes went dull and distant.

"Bunch of bureaucratic liberal bullshit," he repeated.

It felt good to think it, but I'd managed to start into my breathing exercises by then to keep the thoughts from turning into reality, and that's when I forced myself to walk away from him and go back inside the school.

I took a few minutes to cool off, and by the time I got back to the principal's office I could see Donna and Timmy's mother were each holding some pamphlets and other papers, and it turns out that these were the action plans that the principal had mentioned earlier. They were even nodding and smiling and it seemed as if the conversation had been fruitful. Then we all shook hands and walked back to the car.

As we pulled out of the parking lot Timmy's father was still out front smoking a cigarette and leaning against the railing, and from what I could see in the rear view mirror he was staring at us the entire time until we drove from sight.

CHAPTER 8

That night we had dinner with Toby just as we always did, only I didn't have much of an appetite, and I think maybe it had to do with the fact that I was still thinking about my conversation with Timmy's father, and the more I thought back on the things he said and the way he'd acted, the angrier I'd become.

"Look at this, Daddy."

Toby was making a circle in his mashed potatoes and he seemed very proud of this, and even if it wasn't much of an accomplishment, it made me think about how carefree and innocent he was, and then I thought about how he was being picked on by a boy at school, and how that boy's father didn't seem to care, and how he was maybe even contributing to the problem.

I became angrier and angrier and then finally just before dessert I got up from the table and told Donna that I needed to go for a walk because I needed to clear my head and because I didn't much like thinking some of the thoughts that I was thinking so close to Donna and Toby and his mashed potato circle, though I suppose it may have been an ellipse.

Donna asked me if everything was all right, and I told her it was "fine" which was something people generally said when they didn't want to talk and something that I figured Donna would understand since it was what women tended to say when they were unhappy.

Molly trailed me to the front door, and she must have thought that I was going to take her out for a walk, only I knew that I needed to be alone in that moment, so I patted her on the head and quickly stepped outside before she could change my mind by staring at me the way dogs normally do.

It was dark and quiet outside, and the cool night air felt good against my face. I set out walking in no particular direction, and I soon started to think of things other than bullying and "opportunities" and whether action plans could turn children gay.

I'd only just started to feel better when I saw Hayley in the distance with Mister Muggles. I knew it was them because of their outlines and because of the distinct way that Mister Muggles would gyrate when he walked.

I didn't particularly want company, but I decided to

walk in their direction just for something to do and also because it seemed like they were heading in the direction of the park, and I sometimes went there to sit on a swing and relax if there were no people around, and at night there usually weren't.

Hayley wasn't walking on the sidewalk, but was actually walking on the street where it was darker and where they might be struck be a drunk or careless driver. I picked up my pace to say hello and perhaps suggest that they find a safer spot to walk, and that's when I saw Hayley pulling back on the leash and she was saying something to Mister Muggles in a sharp tone, and in that instant all my anger came rushing back.

I started walking faster to see if I could catch up and to ask her why she was doing that, and just then she crossed the street and entered the park where there were no lights at all.

I lost sight of them momentarily but eventually I crossed the road and entered the park at the same spot they had, and soon enough I located them in a sandy playground area where there were swings and a slide and a teeter-totter, and the moment I got close I could again hear her speaking sharply to Mister Muggles, and I saw her pull back hard on his leash once again and the thoughts in my head turned scary, and even though I'd already started into my breathing exercises and knew I should just turn and walk away before something bad happened, my impulses were just too strong, so instead I just walked straight at her.

I could see Mister Muggles was trying to bound forward, and again she yelled at him to sit down and pulled back hard on the leash in a way that made his head snap back and caused him to groan, and by then I could feel my fingernails digging sharply into my hands because I had my fists clenched so hard, and as I got closer I was thinking of Hayley as red and open and my mind was screaming at me to turn away and to consider the consequences of my actions and to consider how good Hayley had always been to Mister Muggles, only it felt as if my body was on auto-pilot by then and there was just no stopping it, but just as I got to within a few feet of them I watched as Hayley dropped to her knees right there in the sand, and she wrapped her arms around Mister Muggles and started sobbing and apologized to him for how she'd been treating him, and in that moment all of the angry, scary feelings that had been coursing through me disappeared in an instant. Then I unclenched my fists and let out a sigh that must have been an audible one, because that's when she finally noticed me.

She drew back in a start but then must have made out my face in the dim light from the moon.

"Are you all right?" I said.

Hayley slowly roused to her feet and wiped her sleeve across the front of her face. It was only when she pulled it away that I saw the large bruise that was covering her eye, and though it looked very much in shape and color like Toby's bruise, I very much doubted that she'd received it roughhousing in a playground.

She said that she was okay, but she was still crying. That was when Mister Muggles bounded forward in my direction, and I knelt down to pet him and to tell him that he was a good boy, which he certainly was, only in that moment I was mostly thinking about the bruise on Hayley's face.

I stood back up and looked her in the eyes, and she looked back at me in a sad way, and maybe as if she were even ashamed.

"Perhaps we should tell Donna?" I said.

Hayley shook her head back and forth rather forcefully at the suggestion. "No, no, it's all right."

"It does not seem all right."

"It's okay, really. It was just a bad night, is all, I never should have…" Only then her voice trailed off, and she didn't finish her sentence.

I had taken a law class in college and had learned that victims often blamed themselves for being hit by their partners for a variety of reasons, but how mostly this was just related to low self-esteem and various other pre-existing issues that were deeply rooted.

"Has it happened before?"

She didn't answer me, which in its own way was an answer.

"He should not place his hands on you."

"It's just when he gets drinking," she said. "He's not like this normally."

"I see."

"He's a good person when he's not drinking. He's just…"

Then her voice trailed off and again she started to cry.

"He's hurting you," I said. I said it because it was true.

Then I took a step forward and placed my hand on her shoulder. I was also thinking about "Get Thee To A Huggery," and though she likely could have benefitted from a hug in that moment, I was in less of a hugging mood than ever, and I thought perhaps it would have been hypocritical for me to do so, given that just moments earlier I was thinking of her as red and open and was wondering how it might be done with only sand around me and my bare hands.

Hayley just stared into my eyes, and I saw a few more tears run down her face, and though she opened her mouth to speak, she must have decided against it, because she didn't say anything after all.

I took my hand from her shoulder and again scrunched down low and scratched behind Mister Muggles' ears as I wondered what kind of monster hurt women—only then I realized what I might have done to Hayley had she not suddenly done what she'd done, and that a slap or a punch was nothing next to a brutal playground murder, and it made me wonder if the real monster was me. Only then I figured we are who we are, and there wasn't much that could be done about it in that moment, so there was no sense beating myself up over it.

CHAPTER 9

I tossed and turned most of the night before getting up early to go to work where I found Gordon already seated at his desk.

"Good morning," he said, without looking up from his screen.

"Good morning," I said, then sat down and turned on my computer.

Last night I'd walked Hayley back home, which I suppose was also walking myself home, and then I went back inside, but only after she begged me not to tell Donna about what had happened. I resisted at first because I didn't much like keeping things from Donna, and I thought that maybe she could even help, but she begged and cried and finally I succumbed and promised for lack of willpower. After that I went inside and tucked Toby into bed and watched as Donna read him a story, then a little after that Donna helped me to achieve it, but then I just lay there and the day's thoughts swelled up in my mind as they sometimes did. I'd tried counting sheep and a few other tricks that my parents had taught me when I was young, but mostly I just thought about Hayley being in an abusive relationship and how I'd read that the children suffered worst of all, and even though they didn't have any actual children, there was still Mister Muggles, and it made me sad to think that he might have to live in such an environment.

I could hear Gordon typing away on his special keypad, so I looked over and it appeared that he was creating some sort of database.

"Can I help you?" he said, even though he didn't look in my direction, and he didn't even break his typing rhythm.

"How did you know that I was looking at you?"

"I'm like a bat, remember?"

Gordon was referring to yesterday when I likened him to a bat for having specially heightened senses. It seemed by his comment that perhaps he held some lingering resentment for what I'd said, but then I couldn't always tell with people, so I decided to just pretend that I hadn't heard it, even though it was quiet and we were the only two people there, and it was obvious to both of us that I had. That's when I looked more closely at his screen, and I could see that the database he was using wasn't the regular company database.

"You've created your own spreadsheet," I said.

"Always do my own," he said.

"I see."

I kept quiet and continued staring at his screen.

"I cluster my contacts by neighborhood," he said. "I try to get people talking to each other to build hype. Even mention their neighbor by name if I can. It stirs up interest. Everyone wants what their neighbor's got, whether it's their car or their wife or their vacuum."

This seemed like an awfully broad claim, but no sooner had he said it than I thought about last year when the McGibbons had purchased their new sports utility vehicle. It was red and shiny and even had a sunroof, and I remembered how a bunch of neighbors had come outside to look at it, even if some of them had only looked from afar, and while I wouldn't say that I wanted Mr. McGibbon's wife or even their new sports utility vehicle, I suppose I might have wanted their vacuum cleaner if they'd had a good one.

"Oh yeah, it's a real racket in the burbs," said Gordon. "The city, too. Most people would rather go broke than let their neighbor have something they can't have. Even if they don't really need it or never really wanted it, they just don't want to give the appearance of not being able to have it."

I couldn't help but wonder if maybe Gordon also had

a subscription to a psychology magazine because he seemed to know a lot about human behavior, but maybe one that was geared more to adults and their buying patterns. At first, all of this seemed far-fetched, but then I thought about how everyone in our neighborhood was buying the ceramic milk cow, or how Donna would often comment if one of our neighbors bought a new purse or a new dress, even though she already had lots of purses and dresses, and so I concluded that Gordon might be onto something.

"People are extremely competitive," he said, "and they always want what they can't have. Just look at the fucking Vortex."

The Vortex was our latest model vacuum, and though I had never heard of it described as "the fucking Vortex," it had a dual engine, and our company claimed that it had been scientifically engineered to suck more dust motes and harmful bacteria than any of our previous vacuums. We were even told by our sales reps that it had enough power to suck a marble through a straw, and this was supposed to feature in our sale pitches to prospective customers. They told us they'd somehow done this in a controlled experiment, though to me it didn't seem possible and I thought that perhaps they were even lying to us, but then I figured I'd probably never know for sure, so there was no point getting too fussed about it.

"You tell people they can't have something new because it's on backorder or sold out and they just go crazy for it. Now you take that same vacuum and tell them it's not only on backorder or sold out but that their neighbor somehow got ahold of one, and they'll be breaking your door down just to get one. I mean it. We're going to need some extra security in here. I may have to hire some private security just to get to my car."

I couldn't tell if Gordon was joking because he wasn't laughing, only I figured he must have been joking because I didn't believe a person in his condition could drive. Only before I could ask him he said, "Watch this," and punched some numbers in his special keypad. A few seconds passed and then someone on the other end must have picked up because he introduced himself and said where he was calling from and a moment later he was telling the person on the phone all about the Vortex and how her neighbor Mrs. Smith had just ordered one and that hers was on backorder, but that if she ordered soon then she might get hers in the next shipment after Mrs. Smith's. This didn't seem particularly truthful, because although they were indeed on order, we were told that they would be available in a few days and that we could order as many as we wanted. Still, the strategy seemed to work because a few minutes later he was taking down her credit card information, and he was smiling and laughing with her before he finally hung up the phone.

"I could sell these all goddamn day," said Gordon after he hung up the receiver, then added, to nobody in particular, "Marble through a mother-fucking straw!"

"I do not believe there is a shortage of vacuums," I said.

"Oh, yeah?"

"No."

"You got any in the back room I don't know about?"

"No," I said.

"You see then, there's a shortage."

"I do not believe that is the truth," I said.

"The truth is just a matter of perspective," said Gordon.

I didn't agree with this statement and was preparing to respond when I saw Mr. Peters coming toward us.

"Early bird catches the worm, eh?" said Peters.

This was a cliché, which was a phrase that was overused or one that betrayed a lack of original thought. Mr. Peters often used trite phrases or clichés in an attempt to motivate his employees. This particular phrase meant that since we'd come in early to work then we were likely to be rewarded, which may have been true since it was hardly morning and Gordon had already made his first sale, so perhaps even a trite or clichéd expression could still be true. But then I thought that maybe it wasn't the early bird that catches the worm but the worm that exaggerates the availability of the Vortex to create a false sense of demand.

"Morning, Frank," said Gordon.

"Good morning, Mr. Peters."

I still couldn't bring myself to call Mr. Peters by his

first name, and so I didn't. He just smiled and tapped the top of our cubicle partition a couple times and then walked away to his office. When I looked back over, I could see that Gordon was looking in my direction.

"Mr. Peters?"

"Yes."

"What, are we on a plantation?"

"No," I said.

"Then why in the hell don't you just call him Frank?"

I was going to explain how my parents taught me to respect authority, but then it seemed like Gordon wasn't really interested because he'd already turned back to his special keypad and was typing in some numbers, and as he did he was shaking his head and mumbling under his breath "Marble through a mother-fucking straw."

CHAPTER 10

On Friday, I arrived home after work and noticed that Josh's truck was in Hayley's driveway. It made me unhappy to see it, but then I figured that Hayley was a grown woman and could make her own decisions in life, even if her decisions were bad ones.

I picked up the mail from the mailbox, and it included that month's issue of *The Child Psychology Magazine*, so I let Molly out into the backyard to do her business and started to read.

There was an article in the new issue called "Blackhawk Down" that talked about the negative impact of helicopter parenting, which was a term used to describe parents who were overprotective of their children and hovered over them so they never fell down or touched germs and things like that. The article said that kids needed contact with germs in order to build up their immune systems and that they needed to get cuts and scrapes or they'd be afraid of the world and wouldn't be able to deal with the slightest pain or discomfort as a grownup. All of this made me think of Timmy's father and what he had said about wrapping our kids in bubble wrap, and though I didn't agree with some of the things he'd said or the way he'd said them, it seemed that there might be some merit to his position, after all. That was the first time that I considered that Donna and I might be helicopter parents by rushing to intervene in the dispute between Toby and Timmy, and that maybe even if our actions didn't alter Toby's sexual orientation, they might still give rise to unintended consequences.

Donna arrived home with Toby soon after, and we all had meatloaf for dinner for the second time that week.

"How was school today?" I said.

Toby shifted in his seat after I asked the question. He was seated up on his knees with his feet tucked beneath him, and although we'd tried to get him to sit up properly, he somehow always reverted back to this position.

"Miss Mullen brought a frog to class."

"Oh, did she?" said Donna, only I already knew about the frog because Donna had told me that he spoke of nothing else during the car ride home.

"I already told you, Mommy."

"Tell me about the frog," I said. This was not solely

to engage my son in conversation, but I was also genuinely interested in the frog. I was also feeling envious because I was thinking back to my own school days, and I couldn't remember a teacher ever bringing a frog to class or any animal for that matter, but then we were also allowed to have peanut butter in classrooms back then, so I figured it was probably a wash.

"He was brown," said Toby, only he didn't say anything more and instead put a small piece of meatloaf into his mouth and began to chew.

"He was a bullfrog," said Donna, "isn't that right?" to which Toby shook his head up and down demonstrably as he chewed, and after some further consideration, I felt that a brown bullfrog in the classroom probably trumped ready access to peanut butter, so I was again feeling envious.

"Miss Mullen put him down on the desk and he hopped around and he even hopped over a pencil," said Toby.

"I see."

"And I got to hold him, and he squirmed like this!" Toby began to squirm in his chair and started to laugh, and I think maybe some bits of meatloaf fell off his fork and onto the floor because I saw Molly run over as soon as it happened.

"But that's not all," said Donna. "Why don't you tell Daddy what you did today?"

Toby's face lit up when she said it, and then he

blurted out, "I got a Spiderman chocolate," with a lot of excitement.

"Where did you get that?" I asked.

Toby straightened up in his chair again and dug his fork back into his meatloaf. He had still not touched his carrots.

"Mommy got it," he said.

"And tell Daddy what you did with it?" she said.

"I gave it," he said.

I'd learned that the way it was with kids is that sometimes they just talked and talked and talked as if there was no end to the words that were in their head and that they were incapable of filtering out what was in their mind versus what they wished to state verbally. Only sometimes kids behaved in exactly the opposite fashion, and they spoke sparingly, and in small, fragmented increments just as Toby was doing now. The April article called "Good Touch, Bad Touch" talked about how this latter approach was common in cases where children were recounting instances of abuse or trauma. However, sometimes they did this where there was no trauma at all, and they were just picking through their meatloaf. This made it difficult to diagnose if a child had gone through some level of abuse or trauma based on their speech, or if they were simply bored with their dinner.

"And who did you give it to?" I asked.

"To Timmy."

"I see."

"And then he ate it up like this," said Toby, and he quickly brought his hand to his mouth and then closed it and puffed out his cheeks. This was Toby's impersonation of Timmy eating the chocolate, and it seemed like a good one.

"What did you and Timmy do then?" said Donna.

Toby shrugged.

"Did you play together after?" she prodded, to which Toby nodded, and then put some more meatloaf in his mouth, even though I think there was still some in there from before.

The way that Donna was asking questions suggested that she knew all the answers before she asked them. I suspected that she must have talked about all of this on the ride home with Toby, or that maybe she had even spoken with Miss Mullen at school.

I also remembered Donna reading some of the action plans to me the night before. One of them talked about doing an unexpected act of kindness to try to win over your adversary, so I suspected that was what they did, and it appeared to have worked.

Part of me was suspicious about bribery being a good way of resolving differences between children, but then I figured that maybe I was looking at it the wrong way and that maybe it wasn't so much bribery but negotiation by means of sharing, and if a Spiderman chocolate was all it took to resolve conflicts between four-year-olds, then maybe I shouldn't be suspicious at all but instead just be thankful, so that's what I decided to be, and then I finished my meatloaf.

❧❧❧

Later that night, I stepped out to the backyard with Molly to let her do her business. We were only outside for a few minutes before I heard some yelling from next door, so I walked over to the fence that separated our house from Hayley's and peeked through one of the cracks, and I could see the light was on in her kitchen and figured that was where the noise must have been coming from. I could barely make out their voices through the windows, but it was clear there was some turmoil because I heard Josh swearing at Hayley and then I think she was yelling for him to leave, and then I heard what sounded like the smashing of glass, and Mister Muggles was barking. I stepped out of our back gate and walked into the grassy laneway between our houses to see if I might get a better look, and though I couldn't see anything, I could hear someone crying and it sounded like a woman's voice. Then I heard the front door open, and a moment later, I saw Josh's truck pull out of the driveway and speed away. I don't believe that he saw me since I remained between our houses and it was already dark out, but either way what was done was done.

I briefly considered going next door to check on Hayley, but then thought better of meddling in her personal business any more than I already had, so instead I just fetched Molly and we went back inside where we stayed in for the night.

I did look outside the window a couple of times before I finally went to bed, and both times I saw the kitchen light still on. It was only after I got up in the middle of the night to go to the bathroom that I checked again and the kitchen light was off.

CHAPTER 11

The next morning, we got up and ate breakfast before Donna took Toby for a playdate with some of his classmates.

Playdates were arrangements negotiated between parents to bring their kids together to play, and since I don't remember having playdates when I was a child, I suppose that either playdates didn't exist back then or else my parents were poor negotiators.

Today's play date would apparently involve pizza and a trip to the movie theater. They left before noon, and then I took Molly for a nice long walk to the park where I'd run into Hayley and Mister Muggles earlier that week.

When we arrived back home, I could see Josh was standing on Hayley's front porch knocking violently on the door with one hand, and I could see him holding flowers in the other. He seemed agitated and was speaking loudly.

"C'mon, open the door. I said I was sorry."

I stood there a moment and watched. Finally, he turned away from the doorway and said "Fucking bitch," under his breath, only he didn't say it far enough under it because I could still hear him.

"Hey man, you see Hayley today?"

"I have not," I said. I said it because it was true.

He turned around and knocked even louder, but still Hayley didn't answer.

"Perhaps she has gone out," I said.

He stood there a while longer as if maybe he were considering this. "You see her car leave?"

"No," I said.

After a moment he stepped off her porch and joined me where I was standing with Molly, only Molly kept her distance. I'd read somewhere once that dogs were just as smart as pigs, if not a shade below, and that they were excellent judges of character, so I couldn't help but wonder if Molly was purposely keeping her distance from Josh because of this, or if she simply hadn't approached him due to fatigue or general apathy.

"You think I can leave these with you?" he said.

I looked down at the flowers in his hand and momentarily felt pity for him, because even though he may have been an abusive alcoholic, I realized that just like me he likely had poor impulse control. I was looking at the flowers and trying to decide what to do when he said, "Or better yet, mind if I come inside and wait for her to come home?"

I looked up and saw him staring hopefully back at me, and though I did not want him to come inside and now wished I'd have just quickly agreed to take his flowers, I also couldn't think of a good enough excuse quickly enough to make him go away. I didn't say anything more and just turned around and walked inside, and he followed right in behind me, kicking off his shoes and exposing his bare feet.

I let Molly off her leash and then led Josh into the kitchen. Before I could invite him to do so, he took a seat at the kitchen table and put the flowers down next to him. Then we simply stared at each other for a moment before I finally asked him if he would like a drink.

"Beer'd be good."

I reached into the fridge for his beer, and then I got one myself for the sake of politeness. After handing him the bottle, he twisted the cap off and immediately consumed nearly half of the contents.

"Where's your lady friend?"

"Donna took Toby to a play date."

"A play date?" he laughed when he said it. "What the fuck is that?"

"It's when parents bring their children together to play."

"That a thing now?"

"Yes," I said.

I remained standing in the kitchen while Josh remained seated. He then lifted his bare feet up and put them on the chair beside him and looked out the large kitchen window toward Hayley's house. Something about this bothered me, though I couldn't say for sure if it was him putting his bare feet up on one of our seat cushions or the fact that he seemed to be looking for movement next door, though it's possible it was some combination of the two.

"Do you have to work today?" I asked, trying my best to make small talk.

"Got the day off," he said.

"I see."

He then polished off his bottle and placed it down on the kitchen table. "Got another one?"

I handed him a second bottle, and he twisted the top off and took another long drink.

Even before we'd come inside the house, I could smell the odor of alcohol on Josh's breath, and I concluded that Hayley was correct and that Josh did indeed have a problem with alcohol. This made me think of the July issue of *The Child Psychology Magazine* because there was an article inside called "Find your Freud." It was an article about the benefits of counseling and how the right psychiatrist, psychologist, or otherwise educated person could make an invaluable difference in your child's life.

The article said that most any problem can be cured by the right counseling, and though the article was geared more toward bedwetting and defiance and a broad range of youthful neuroses, I figured it would likely work just as well for Josh if he found the right psychiatrist, psychologist, or otherwise educated person. I thought about suggesting this to him, but then I didn't know him very well and didn't particularly like him, so I decided not to.

"What is it that you and Hayley fought about?"

Josh took another swig "She doesn't like when I drink," he said.

"Why is that?"

"She says I get ornery." He dragged out this last word and made a funny face as he said it.

"Do you believe she is right?" I asked.

Josh looked over at me with a serious expression. "What're you, a cop?"

"No," I said.

He stared at me for a couple seconds with the same serious expression and then suddenly his face went from serious to laughing. "Nah, man, I'm just fucking with you," he said, then he looked back out the window toward Hayley's house. "I don't think I'm any worse than anyone else when they drink. Nothing special about me. Never met a girl before who thinks her shit stinks less than that one."

"I believe she has been in some bad relationships before."

"Who hasn't?" he said.

A few moments later he'd finished the second bottle of beer. This time he didn't even ask, but just stood up and walked to the fridge where he pulled out another beer. I had barely taken three sips from mine and concluded that his drinking problem was significant.

"Do you believe that you drink too much?"

Josh finished another long sip and then he looked at me again with a serious look, only this time his face didn't move back to laughing. "You fucking serious?"

"Yes," I said.

"Look, where the fuck do you get off..." Then he stopped, and I saw his eyes starting to well up.

"If it is a problem, perhaps you should seek help."

Josh stood silently in the kitchen and then a moment later drew one of his hands up to his eyes, and it looked like he might cry. "Perhaps she should just stop being such a fucking cunt," he said.

I didn't appreciate Josh's language or how he was talking about Hayley, and I was just about to ask him to leave when he looked at me and said, "Why the fuck does everything have to be so goddamned hard?" and then he started crying for real, and I didn't know what to do.

I watched him sobbing in my kitchen and was wondering what to do or say next. That's when I thought of "Get Thee To A Huggery" and the healing effects that hugs had on children, and even though I didn't much like Josh, I could see that he was in pain, and before I thought about it any further, I stepped forward and embraced him in a hug and told him that things would get better. Unfortunately, there was something about this that offended him because he immediately pushed me back where I fell hard against the counter.

"What're you, a fucking queer?"

I didn't respond because it seemed more like an accusation, and he also seemed very angry. My back hurt from where it had hit the counter, and I could see the rage boiling up in his eyes, and I could see out the corner of my eye that Molly had just come into the room to see what was happening.

The next thing I knew, Josh lunged forward and he had one of his hands hard around my throat and he'd pinned my head down on the counter making it difficult to breath. Everything seemed to slow down in that moment, and he was calling me a "weirdo" and a "faggot" as he had his hands around my throat and neck, and I heard Molly barking wildly in the background, only her barks seemed to be coming at me from a distance and through an echo. And I could feel his nails digging into the back of my neck and that's when I opened my eyes and reached out to grab the first object I could find, so I grabbed a ceramic ashtray and smashed it against his head, shattering it all around us.

Josh drew back a step, and I could see that he was bleeding near one of his ears, only then he lunged forward at me again, and this time wrapped both his hands around my neck, only by then I'd already reached for a knife from the chopping block on the counter, so I started to stab him in the gut and kept saying "Stop," over and over and over again, only he didn't stop, so I kept stabbing and stabbing and stabbing until my entire hand was red and wet and covered in blood, and I didn't stop until I was sufficiently certain he was sufficiently dead.

CHAPTER 12

As it turned out, it wasn't a glass ashtray at all but the ceramic glass cow that I had used to smash Josh's head open, and it made me wonder why the thought of an ashtray flashed into my mind at all since neither Donna or I were smokers and since I don't believe we even owned an ashtray, but then I figured the brain was a funny thing and who knows why it thinks the things it does.

By then I was also thinking about the coincidence of using the very item that Hayley and Josh had brought as a gift the previous weekend to defend myself, and then I thought how it was fortunate that Hayley had been inspired to purchase the ceramic cow by seeing it at the McGibbons' house, and I figured that if the McGibbons had never bought a ceramic milk dispensing cow, then maybe Hayley would have purchased something soft or innocuous that I couldn't have used as a weapon, and how maybe I would be the one dead on the floor now, and it would be Josh having all of these thoughts, only his thoughts would probably be different. Only then I figured there were thousands of permutations that could have gone differently had Hayley never seen the McGibbons' ceramic cow, like maybe she would have broken up with Josh or gotten into a car accident or won the lottery, so I figured there wasn't much point dwelling on the possibilities.

Once I came to my senses, I let Molly into the backyard to keep her from the mess, and then I drew the blinds around the sun porch in the kitchen so I could do what had to be done in privacy.

I carried him into the garage, which thankfully had a connecting door from inside the house. Then I started cutting him up right there on the garage floor where I'd laid out some garbage bags, and as I did I was thinking about the last time I used the hacksaw, and it was to make Toby a small tree fort in the backyard, and though I didn't much like the idea of using the same tool that I used to make Toby's tree fort to cut up a dead body and conceal a murder, I only thought of this after I'd cut off his head and one of his arms, so I figured there was no point changing to a different tool by then.

After it was done, I placed him into several fresh

garbage bags that had drawstrings and were guaranteed not to leak according to the commercials. Donna had purchased these new premium bags, and while I'd originally doubted the extra features would justify the cost, I couldn't help but think about the peace of mind it now brought to know the bags were heavy duty and leak proof.

I cleaned up the kitchen and the garage as best I could with bleach and other cleaners and a hose and finally took a shower and then placed all of the bloody clothes and cleaning rags and hacksaw into a fourth garbage bag, along with his shoes. I then went outside and drove my car into the garage where I lined the trunk with newspaper just in case there was seepage, and finally I loaded the four garbage bags into the back.

This was the first person I had killed in nearly five years, and even though I felt this one was mostly in self-defense and that maybe I could have gone to the authorities and tried to offer an innocent explanation, I also figured this would bring a lot of uncomfortable questions and that at the end of the day it would be only my word about what had happened and how maybe they wouldn't believe me, and I wasn't willing to take that chance. I would probably also have to hire a lawyer to defend me, and from what I'd learned in my law class in college this could cost as much as our house, and no matter how many vacuums I sold there would be no way I could manage that, and so I figured the cost of a few premium garbage bags and a hacksaw was more cost efficient than hiring a lawyer, so that is what I did.

I immediately drove to the garbage dump, which was the same place I'd disposed of my landlord five years before, and even though I figured it was risky to do so in the middle of the day on a Saturday, I also felt the risk was too great to leave cut up pieces of Hayley's boyfriend along with the murder weapon and murder clothes in my trunk, so there was no sense beating myself up over it.

I parked nearby and waited in my car for nearly twenty minutes to ensure that I was completely alone. Only then did I get out of the car and dispose of the garbage bags in something of a landfill. I tossed a few other pieces of garbage on top of him to make sure he was well covered, then I got back into my car and drove home.

It was nearly dinnertime as I pulled into the driveway. I saw that Donna and Toby were already back from their playdate, and as I parked my car I felt an immediate sense of dread that maybe I'd missed a splotch of blood or bone, and that if Toby stumbled across it, it might have some lingering effects on him, and that soon enough he'd be seeing a psychiatrist, psychologist, or otherwise educated person of his own.

I stepped inside the house and Molly came running up to me and wagging her tail excitedly, which was something that dogs do when they are excited that their master has come home, or someone they know has come home, or anyone comes home for that matter.

Then, in the next instant, I saw Donna walk in from the kitchen, and before I could even take off my shoes, she'd run toward me and grabbed me in a big hug.

"They're beautiful," she said, kissing my cheeks.

I just looked at her blankly because I had no idea what she was talking about. Then she led me by the hand into the kitchen to show me a vase of flowers, and only then did I realize that these were Josh's flowers for Hayley, and that in the heat of the moment, I had entirely forgotten them there on the kitchen table, and that Donna must have presumed incorrectly that I had purchased them for her.

"What did I do to deserve these?" she said.

I told her that she was a good partner and mother without saying anything more because I didn't much like lying to Donna or anybody else, and since what I said was true, I felt that I wasn't really lying to her at all and that if she extrapolated what I'd said as relating to the flowers, I figured that was her own business and nothing to get fussed about.

Donna leaned in and sniffed them and asked me if I'd smelled them. I answered "No" which was the truth, so then I leaned in and smelled them. That's when I noticed the card in the flowers, and it just said "I Love You" with a smiley face beneath in blue pen, and even though it wasn't my handwriting, I felt as if Donna must not have noticed.

"So what have you been up to all day?" she asked.

By then, she was washing some strawberries in the sink.

Donna had a singsong tone in her voice and I could see that the flowers had made her very happy, and even though I hadn't actually purchased the flowers, it made me happy to see it.

"I've been busy," I said, and hoped that would be the end of it.

"Oh yeah, doing what?"

"I cleaned up a bit and took some garbage out," I said. I said it because it was true.

I could see when I said it that she looked around a bit at the kitchen, and she must have noticed that things were very much the same as they were before, and although it wasn't much of an explanation, I figured that she might not question it too much, and as it turns out, she didn't.

After Donna went back to washing her strawberries, I walked into the den to find Toby playing with some Lego. We had to take the Lego away from him for a few months because he'd put a small piece up his nose and we'd had to visit the doctor, but now that he was a little older, we felt that he could be trusted.

"Daddy, look!" he said, pointing to some sort of castle.

It wasn't much of a castle. The structure was too small and was poorly conceived, but at least it had a moat and some trees so that much was decent.

"That is very nice," I said. As a general rule, I tried to lie to people as little as possible, though I made the exception for my son because I'd read various articles in *The Child Psychology Magazine* that children benefited from positive reinforcement, even where it was undeserved, and it could even stunt their creativity or confidence if you undermined their work.

"This man goes here, and this one goes here," said Toby.

Just like the castle, it wasn't much of a formation. He'd arranged his knights outside the castle walls, and even though I felt that the men would be much safer inside, I once again said "That's very nice," even if the fact of the matter was that it was a tactically poor decision and would likely lead his men to slaughter. My mind had also drifted by that point because I was worried that if I'd missed something as obvious as a bouquet of flowers that I might have missed something else significant. As a result, I stood up and went back to the kitchen where Donna was making dinner. I scanned the area briefly before Donna started talking.

"So where were you anyway?" she said.

"I just went for a drive," I said, and I felt this was mostly true.

"Why didn't you take Molly?" she asked. "We found her out in the backyard when we got home."

I wasn't sure how to answer this. Like the flowers, I had completely forgotten about Molly being outside in the backyard. Finally, I just answered with a generalized ambiguous phrase that "She loves to play outside," which might not have been much of an answer, but it was one that happened to be true.

Both Toby and I then took exhaustion naps after dinner, though I suppose mine might have also had some trauma nap mixed in. We then watched some television, and later that night Donna helped me to achieve it with her mouth, which was probably her way of thanking me for the flowers, but whatever the motivation, it ended up being a pleasant way to end the evening, and even though I couldn't help thinking about how badly things had gone that day, I also couldn't help thinking, at least in that moment, that they hadn't gone all the way bad.

CHAPTER 13

The following day, I took Molly for a walk when I discovered Hayley standing on the sidewalk in front of the McGibbons' house, which was just a few houses up from ours.

"Good morning," I said.

"Good morning."

I could see that the bruise over her eye had started to heal.

"I'm sorry about yesterday," she said.

I asked her what she meant by that.

"I mean, what with Josh banging on my door and all. I saw you two talking."

I felt a lump in my throat the moment she said it. I tried to swallow it away, only after a couple swallows, it was still there, so I figured it really wanted to be there and there was no point resisting. "He seemed upset," I said.

"We had just an awful fight last night. He'd been drinking. He smashed some glasses. It was awful. I told him to get out and not come back."

"I see."

"He came over the next day with some flowers, but I wouldn't let him in. He'd been drinking, I could tell."

"That was probably wise," I said.

"Funny though—" She then stopped mid-sentence, and that's when I noticed why she was standing where she was, because Josh's truck was parked on the road in front of the McGibbons' house. "This is his truck. He must have left it here for some reason."

"Perhaps because he had been consuming alcohol," I said.

"Yeah, that hasn't really stopped him before."

I hadn't taken into consideration that Josh had driven. In hindsight, I remembered seeing his truck around from time to time parked on the street. Sometimes he would park it in the driveway and other times he would just park it on the road as he must have done yesterday. I hadn't even thought to look for his vehicle or to go through his pockets for his keys or wallet.

"Did you see which way he went yesterday?"

"I really couldn't say," I said.

She hesitated after I said this, as if she had something more to add, and after a moment she did.

"The thing is, I was sort of spying out the window. I saw you and him talking on your driveway, and it seemed like maybe he'd walked off with you, toward your porch or something?"

"We did speak briefly by my porch," I said, and I felt that this was mostly the truth, even if I'd left out the part that most of our speaking had actually occurred a little bit past the porch in the kitchen where I would later murder him with a knife.

"Did he mention where he was going?" she asked.

"No," I said, and this was true.

"Strange."

I could tell that Hayley was feeling uneasy, only I didn't get the sense that she was feeling uneasy about me as much as she was uneasy about the fact that Josh could still be lurking nearby.

"I nearly called the police," she said. "I had the phone in my hand when I saw that you'd shown up to distract him."

I nodded because I had no reason not to believe her.

"This is just so embarrassing." She then put both her hands up to her face and I thought she might cry again, only she didn't.

"You have no reason to feel embarrassed," I said.

And then she removed her hands from her face and nodded and said, "Yeah, I know, I know," even though it seemed to me as if maybe she didn't really believe it. Finally, she said, "Look, if you see him around, can you please let me know?"

I told her I would, and this was very easy to commit to because I knew it would require little effort on my part.

After that, we parted ways, and I realized that eventually Josh would be declared missing and that the police would surely come around looking for him, and that it would be a logical place to start where his truck had been abandoned, and given that Hayley had seen us together I figured it was only a matter of time before they came around talking to me and Donna and asking a lot of uncomfortable questions. This had happened to me once before when my landlord had gone missing, but given that I was never arrested or placed in jail, I felt that my answers must have all been pretty good, so I figured that if I just did the same as I'd done before then hopefully everything would work out just fine.

CHAPTER 14

I went to work on Monday just as I always did, only I couldn't help lingering momentarily at the sight of Josh's truck before I pulled out of the driveway.

I was still thinking about it when I walked to my desk. As usual, Gordon had arrived ahead of me, and he was already on the phone with a customer by the time I sat down.

"Look, ma'am, you've never seen power like this before. To be perfectly honest, I'm not even sure I can sell it to you. You're going to need to tell me who laid your carpet. If it wasn't tacked down just right, The Vortex is going to pull it right up off the ground. Yeah, that's right. No, ma'am, I can't sell it to you without that assurance. No, I'm not kidding. We're talking about liability here."

He paused just long enough to look in my direction

and smile. I'd found that for a sufficiently blind person
Gordon interacted with me in much the same way as any
regular person might. I'd also noticed that ever since I'd
read the January issue of *The Child Psychology Magazine*
I'd started thinking and using the word "sufficiently"
with much more frequency. I'd found this was the case
with certain words and phrases, and that once they got
stuck in your head it was hard to get them out, and I figured this was just another one of those times.

"All right then, you call me back with the name of
the installer and the year it went in, and I'll check with
our R and D department and get back to you. I'm just a
little concerned though. Just a little concerned that The
Vortex might be too powerful. All right ma'am, you have
my number then. You call me back when you can." Gordon then clicked off the call. "You see that? That's just
what I'm talking about. She starts debating the power of
the vacuum, so I tell her it's probably too powerful for
her carpet and that maybe she can't have it. Now she
wants it bad. She'll be calling me back before the end of
the day."

"I do not believe we've ever had a vacuum that lifted
up someone's carpet," I said.

"Yeah, well, that may be a chance you're willing to
take, but I bet it's not a chance Ms. McGillivray wants to
take."

"I do not believe you are being truthful with the customers."

"You saying it's impossible a strong vacuum could lift carpet?"

"Nothing is impossible," I said.

"Exactly."

"But it is not likely," I said.

"You willing to bet your house on it?"

"No," I said.

"Exactly." Then Gordon turned back to his computer and started going through his contacts.

It didn't feel right to me that Gordon was misleading customers, especially since this was only his second week on the job, and I briefly thought about speaking with Mr. Peters about it, only then I thought about how I'd slain my neighbor's boyfriend and buried him in a landfill, so I thought that maybe it wasn't the worst behavior after all, and that perhaps it was hypocritical of me to be so judgmental.

"Don't you pout over there," said Gordon.

I said that I wasn't.

"Yeah, but I can hear it."

I did not believe this was true since I wasn't making any noise.

"Look," said Gordon, "let me tell you something, just so there's no hard feelings. Maybe I fudged the likelihood the carpet would come up, sure, but can you say for sure it couldn't happen? Let me tell you, I've heard just about everything there is to hear in this world, and nothing surprises me anymore. Nothing. Did you hear how my old company let us all go?"

"Not very much," I said.

"So we all get to work on Saturday morning, an hour before the store opens, so we can set-up. Only nobody's setting up, and there's someone there from human resources standing with the bosses."

I was listening intently. I had heard about the company closing but had not heard many of the details.

"They wait for everyone to show up, and then the lady from human resources tells us that the company has been dissolved, and that we are all out of a job. No notice. No nothing."

"I see."

"That ain't the half of it," said Gordon. "Then she starts telling us about the shitty severance packages they are offering, only suddenly she stops, with a big smile on her face, and she says 'This may take a while, but don't worry, the company has been authorized to order fish and chips for everyone, for lunch.' We've all just lost our jobs, and she's up there talking about fish and fucking chips."

Gordon said it was like that all over the company, in every store, only some of the stores ordered tacos instead of fish and chips.

"I took all the tartar sauce when I left," he said.

Like his comment about needing extra security, I couldn't tell for sure if Gordon was being truthful, only it seemed as if he was. Then he said, "And if a whole company can be fired like that, you really think it's so impossible a strong vacuum cleaner might lift up an old carpet?"

Then Gordon went back to his computer to look through his contacts. He didn't say anything else to me, except I saw him shaking his head at his screen, and he kept mumbling under his breath "Fish and motherfucking chips."

❧❧❧

I sold three vacuums that day, and although that was a decent amount, Gordon was able to sell seven, and one of those was even to Ms. McGillivray, who had indeed called back just as Gordon expected, at which time she provided him the information about her carpet. Even then, he'd told her that he would have to confirm with his manager that the Vortex would be safe for her home, and then he put the call on hold and laid the phone down on his desk for three minutes while he somehow played Spider Solitaire on his computer before finally picking the phone back up and telling her that he had good news.

While at first it had bothered me that Gordon was seemingly being dishonest with the customers, the more I thought about it, the more I felt it wasn't all that different from all the psychological tricks and strategies the company had taught us about closing sales. The company had

told us that there were a number of different ways that
you could trick people into purchasing something they
didn't really need or want, and even if they didn't use
those exact words to describe what they did, that was
more or less the gist of it.

One of these tactics was called "The Columbo
Close." It was named after a television show from the
seventies, and though the main character was a detective
and not a vacuum salesman, our company apparently felt
there were sufficient similarities between their styles to
incorporate him into our sales strategies.

The Columbo Close was all about taking advantage
of people when their guard was down. He would lull his
suspects into a false sense of security, and even say
goodbye or goodnight depending on what time of day it
was, before suddenly turning around and saying "Oh, just
one more thing," and it was in that very moment after the
suspect had exhaled and felt they were out of jeopardy
that they were most suggestible. We were trained to tell
people who were hemming and hawing that the item
might not be in stock, which lowered their guard, but that
we could check and see if it was, and then just before we
put them on hold to check, we'd pause and ask if they'd
like us to place one on hold if it was still available. When
we did this, an inordinate number of people would say
yes. It worked even better in our retail stores, where the
salesperson could actually turn around after a few steps
of walking away and say "Oh, would you like me to bring

one out if I have one?" and the person would often say yes, therefore psychologically committing to the purchase. We were told the "Oh" or the "Hey" at the start was particularly important because it signified that things were very informal and light and easy.

The Columbo Close was just one of many ways we used psychological warfare to convince customers to purchase our products. There were others such as "The Assumptive Close" or "The Alternative Close" or "The Benjamin Franklin Close," and to me they all involved some form of trickery or deceit against the customer, so at the end of the day I figured that maybe this was just Gordon's own spin on things, and so I didn't think any more of it.

By then, I was also trying to figure out how he was able to play spider solitaire when he was mostly blind, only I didn't want to bring it up because he'd reacted sensitively the last time I mentioned blindness or compared him to a bat, and since most spiders were black just like bats, I felt it was probably a topic that was best to be avoided.

CHAPTER 15

"What is that, honey?"

It was Tuesday night and we'd just eaten dinner. Donna and I were putting away the dishes and Toby was crawling around on the floor with a toy car making childish car-like noises.

Ever since Toby had been a toddler, Donna had used the name "honey" interchangeably for both of us, so it wasn't immediately clear who she was talking to, which to me seemed to be a failing of precision on Donna's part. Only then I saw Donna walk over to where Toby was, and that cemented the fact that she must have been talking to him, which made sense because at the moment she said it I was holding a potato masher, and it would have been awfully strange if Donna had not known what that was, and I might have even felt it degraded her intelligence to ask that question, so I was happy not to have had to degrade her intelligence in my mind.

That's when I looked down and saw Toby holding a small piece of white ceramic in his hand, and even though I'd tried to be as thorough and diligent as I could in cleaning up the murder scene, I'd also been mindful that Donna and Toby could come home anytime from the play date, so I'd probably gone a little faster than I would have liked.

"What is that?" she said, kneeling down beside him. Donna took the object out of Toby's hand and looked at it curiously from a few angles.

"Honey, is this a piece from Hayley's gift?"

I figured this was certainly my turn at being "Honey" because Toby was only four and surely had no idea Hayley had even purchased us a gift, let alone what gift, so I concluded correctly that Donna was speaking to me. And even though it was rather an obvious conclusion and not much of a feat, I still felt some small satisfaction that I'd interpreted this correctly and easily as Donna turned in my direction waiting for a response.

I walked over after drying my hands and took the object from her and turned it over a few times just as Donna had. I did this to perpetuate the ruse that I was just as puzzled as she was, when in fact, I knew that she was correct and that this certainly was a piece of the ceramic white cow that everyone in our neighborhood was now purchasing because of the McGibbons. It was also clearly from the cow because even though it was a small piece, it had one of the cow's tiny udders, so I figured there was no sense lying about it.

"It would appear to be a piece of the ceramic cow," I said.

Then Donna walked over to the counter where it had previously been, and I watched her look in a few cabinets and then finally she turned in my direction. "What the hell happened?" she said.

I preferred her not to swear in front of Toby because I'd read in "Monkey See, Monkey Do" that children were much like monkeys in how they imitated others, and if they were exposed to words and actions just a few times they might absorb and adopt the behavior as their own. Thankfully, Donna had only said the word one time, so I figured that a moment's indiscretion likely wouldn't alter Toby's dialogue. "It would appear that the cow has been broken," I said.

"You think?" she said, only she said it sarcastically.

"Yes."

"And how the hell did that happen?" she said, with both her hands on her hips, which was just how the women behaved on most of the television shows and movies that I watched when they weren't happy with their partners. I thought about mentioning how stereotypically she was acting and thought that maybe she'd get a laugh out of it, and it would create some levity in the situation, and then maybe we'd all laugh together and maybe she would even forget about the ceramic cow. Only there was probably just as good of a chance the comment would just make her angrier, which usually made for worse days and nights, so instead I decided to feign ignorance and responded, "How could I possibly know," which was a generalized ambiguous answer that sometimes worked to distract attention. Only it didn't work this time because I could see that she still had both her hands on her hips.

"Well, I sure as hell didn't break it," she said, "did you?"

This was now the third time she'd said "hell," and I figured by then that Toby might finally have absorbed it, and I started thinking about how this had increased the possibility that Toby might one day tell his teacher to "go to hell" or that he might state "what in the hell is this" during show and tell if one of his classmates brought in something ridiculous, and how he'd likely be sent to the principal's office in either scenario and perhaps from then on be pegged as one of the bad kids, and maybe even be held back a grade if the delinquency continued. And then I figured this might hamper his future education or job prospects, and that this in turn could spiral into substance abuse and indigence and a whole host of issues.

"When would I have broken it?" I asked.

This was the closest I could come to answering her without full-out lying, which was something I avoided whenever possible. That was when Donna knelt down

next to Toby and asked if he'd broken the cow, which
seemed at first like an outrageous proposition because
Toby couldn't possibly reach the counter, and how even
the smartest monkey or four-year-old was still rather stupid when compared to adults, so he would surely never
be able to sweep up and dispose of this sort of mess.
Then I wondered if maybe Donna saw something in Toby
that I didn't, such as some extra intelligence or capability
that I hadn't perceived, only then I thought back to the
uneven mashed potato boat and the poorly conceived
Lego castle and how he would sometimes even defecate
in his own pants, and the thought of extra intelligence left
my mind.

Toby just shook his head without even looking at
her, and then went back to playing with his toy car and
making "vroom, vroom" noises, which seemed to further
illustrate the point I had previously been making in my
head.

"Who else has been in here since last weekend?" said
Donna.

I couldn't think of anyone else who'd been in here
except for Josh on Saturday, and I knew I couldn't mention that for obvious reasons. Only then I thought back to
how drunk he was when he and Hayley had come for
dinner.

"Perhaps Josh knocked it over," I said, "and was too
embarrassed to tell anyone."

I could tell that Donna was seriously considering this

because she suddenly became very quiet, and I could even see her tongue pushing out the bottom of her lip, which was something she did when she was deep in thought.

"But I'm sure I'd seen it since then," she said.

I said that I didn't recall seeing it since then, which was an outright lie, but one I felt was necessary to tell in the circumstances in an effort to trick Donna into doubting herself on that particular point, and I could see that my lie had the intended effect, because she finally resigned herself to the fact that Josh must have knocked it over in his drunken state.

I didn't much like tricking Donna like this, nor did I feel it was right to blame Josh for breaking the ceramic cow, but then I figured that since he'd attacked me in my own kitchen, and I'd used the ceramic cow to defend myself from his attack, then maybe in a way he actually was responsible for the breaking of the ceramic cow after all, so in a weird way I felt that none of this was really much of a lie at all.

"It's just the strangest thing," she said before throwing the fragment into the garbage and returning to the dishes.

I went back to helping her, too, only I wasn't thinking about dishes or ceramic cows or anything related to Josh. Instead, I was thinking about Toby and how he probably wasn't all that gifted based on all the evidence at hand. But rather than lamenting the fact that Toby was just a normal four-year-old child, I couldn't help but think of all the child prodigies who'd been forced into grueling academic schedules or chess tournaments or the entertainment industry, and how many of them had spiraled into substance abuse issues and indigence and a whole host of other issues.

I was just recognizing the paradox of it all when Donna handed me the salad bowl, and that caused me to think about a whole host of other things.

CHAPTER 16

I arrived home Wednesday after work and parked in the driveway just as I always did, only once I got out of the car, I took a few steps toward Josh's truck and wondered how much longer it would be parked there before it was ticketed or towed or otherwise disposed of in some fashion.

I was just about to turn around and go inside when I saw a man stand up from the other side of the truck.

"Hey, mate!"

I turned around hoping that he might be speaking to somebody else, but as it turned out I was the only one standing there, so I figured that he must have been speaking to me, unless perhaps he was a crazy man who was speaking to some imaginary person, only I figured that I couldn't hope to be that lucky. I didn't answer until he stepped out from behind the truck and took a few steps toward me.

"You there, hello?"

By then, I knew he was speaking to me, so I figured I had to answer him. He was about middle-aged and was wearing a beige trench coat even though it wasn't all that cold out.

"Hello," I said.

He moved closer to where I was on the sidewalk, and I could see that he was basically my height, and it looked like he hadn't shaved for a few days, and as he got even closer, I could see that there was some gray mixed into his stubble, which was interesting because there wasn't any gray in his actual hair.

"Hell of a nice neighborhood, eh, mate?"

I nodded because it was true.

"Hell of a nice neighborhood," he repeated, "that's what I thought the moment I saw it, 'there's a hell of a nice neighborhood if there ever was one,' isn't that right, mate? There's a good mate."

He spoke with a strong English accent, only I wasn't thinking about that so much as I was thinking about how glad I was that Toby wasn't around because I figured if Donna's bad language hadn't settled into him by that point, it likely would have solidified after listening to this man.

"So you live here, do you?"

I could see he had some perspiration on his forehead, but he didn't make any effort to wipe it away. "I do," I said, "right here on the corner." Then I pointed to our house.

"Well, isn't that something," he said. "Beautiful house, chap."

I had no idea who this person was, but he seemed very friendly.

"It is," I said. Then added, "Donna's parents helped us with the down payment."

He looked at me a bit curiously when I said it.

"This Donna," he said, "that your wife, mate?"

"I live with her," I said.

"Ah yes, that's a good setup what you've got there, ain't it, mate? There's a good mate."

I'd never been called a good mate before, but it seemed to be something he liked to say.

"Now if you don't mind me saying, mate, I couldn't help notice you took a good butcher's at this truck here." He turned his attention back to Josh's pickup, only I didn't respond because I didn't know how. "Got a good look at this truck, didn't you, mate?"

"Yes," I said, because I didn't see any need to deny it.

"Sure is a nice truck, isn't it? Always wanted one just like it, but the missus wouldn't have it. That's what the missus always said, that she'd have none of it. That's what the missus said." I just looked at him, and he continued. "Reckon you must feel the same way about this truck here, eh, chap? There's a good chap."

He seemed to have some difficulty between choosing to call me mate or chap.

"I see that it has been parked here for a while," I said.

"Indeed," he said. "And if I may ask, did you happen to notice when it was first parked here?"

It seemed odd to me that a stranger would take such an interest in Josh's truck, but then he seemed friendly enough by complimenting our home and calling me mate and chap, so I figured there was no harm in answering him, so I did. "I believe it has been parked here since the weekend," I said.

"Since the weekend," he repeated. "I don't suppose you recall which day, exactly, eh, mate? There's a good mate."

"No," I said.

He paused when I said it, then he finally reached up and wiped the sweat from his brow. "Very curious," he said after a moment.

"I suppose."

"And do you know whose truck this is?" he asked.

"I believe it belongs to Josh," I said.

"Josh, you say?" he said it as if it were a surprise, only he didn't seem like he was all the way surprised.

"Yes," I said.

"And would you happen to know Josh's last name, mate?"

I shook my head. I was wondering who this person was to be asking me all these questions. Finally, I asked him if he lived in the neighborhood.

"Oh, I suppose I do, in a way, mate."

This seemed like an intentionally ambiguous answer, so I asked him which house he lived in.

"Oh, you can't see it from here. You can't quite see it quite from here. Wish you could, though. Beautiful neighborhood. Need to find a neighborhood just like this, that's what I tell the missus."

I felt that he was being purposely evasive, so I said goodbye and turned to go inside when the man called out after me.

"Oh, if I could just trouble you a moment longer," he said.

I turned around and could see by then that he'd taken a few steps closer.

"Could you tell me how you knew this man? This Josh fella?"

"He was dating my neighbor," I said.

"Yes, I see," and he looked directly over to Hayley's house, so presumably he knew which neighbor I was speaking about.

"Are you a police officer?" I asked.

He looked at me curiously. "And now why would you ask that? I look that much like a bobbie, do I mate?"

I told him that Hayley had been concerned about Josh coming around and that she had nearly called the police because of it, and it was easy to say all of this because all of this was true. Then he got a smile on his face and pointed his finger at me, but it was a friendly point.

"Very clever, mate. Very clever, indeed. There's a good mate."

I didn't believe it was particularly clever, but I thanked him nonetheless. He then introduced himself as a detective and said that he was searching for Josh as he had been declared a missing person. I also noticed that he'd shifted from calling me "chap" to "mate" on a more regular basis, and I wondered if there was any tangible difference between the two, but before I could ask him, he'd already moved on to a new question.

"It would seem that he has not gone to work the past few days," said the detective.

I was surprised by this. Not because he hadn't shown up for work, because I surely would have been shocked if he had, but because I'd figured that "roofing" had just been a euphemism for "unemployed." However, it seemed that Josh did, in fact, have a job.

"So you say that he was dating your neighbor, do you?"

"Yes," I said.

"Very curious," he said. "Very curious indeed."

I didn't see what was so curious about it. Then I said so.

"Well, you see, sir, it is puzzling why you would say that he 'was' dating your neighbor, rather than that he 'is' dating your neighbor. Said it twice now, haven't you, mate?"

I could see now that he was already suspicious of me.

"I do not understand why it is puzzling," I said.

"Of course, old chap, of course. Let me explain. You see, you have described it as if he is not coming back, that is all. Maybe just a slip of the tongue, eh, mate? There's a good mate with a slip of the tongue."

"No," I said.

"No?"

"No," I repeated.

"All right, mate. There's a good mate if I ever saw one."

I didn't respond because I wasn't sure how.

"So then," he continued, "you believe that he is coming back, then, after all?"

I could tell that the detective was trying to trap me with my answers. It had also occurred to me that all of his serious questions had come after I had turned around to go home, and this made me think of the Columbo Close, and though I wanted to ask him if he'd seen the show and maybe was deploying this as a strategy, I felt that now wasn't the time or place to do so.

"How could I possibly know?" is all I said. Then when he didn't say anything further I again turned to go home and that's when he called out once more.

"I'm still having trouble with something, though. Still just a wee bit confused on a point. Maybe if you helped me along a bit, it might get me back to the missus in time for dinner. Gets me no favors if I come home late for dinner. You know the type, don't you, mate? There's a good mate."

"I have to get home," I said.

"Right you do, and would never dream to stop you, would never dream of it. But if you might just humor me a spell. That's what the missus does, humors me, you know. Could I ask you a question, then mate?"

"Yes," I said.

"Hate to belabor the point. Hate to do it, old chap. But you say that he *was* dating your neighbor."

"Yes."

"Then what makes you believe they are no longer dating?" he said.

"Because Hayley told me so."

"She told you so?" he said with a rather puzzled expression on his face.

"Yes."

"And when did she do that, if you don't mind helping out an old bobbie, trying to do his best to make an honest living?"

I found the question oddly worded, and he didn't seem particularly old, but I answered him anyway.

"Very good, very good, mate. There's a good mate.

This answers a great deal. It answers a great deal indeed."

The detective didn't say anything further, so I said goodbye and walked back toward the house, and this time he didn't call after me as I did.

As I stepped inside the house, and Molly rushed forward to greet me, I couldn't help but think about how pleasant the detective was, and I also couldn't help wonder if maybe he really did think I was a good mate, and so I became optimistic that this was just a chance encounter and that I wouldn't see him again.

CHAPTER 17

We saw it reported in the local news the next day as a missing person case. I could see a look of alarm on Donna's face when she saw it on the television.

"Can you believe this?" she said.

"Yes."

Toby was playing on the ground with some toys, and Molly was sprawled out asleep beside him.

"He was just sitting across from us, not more than a week ago."

"Yes," I said.

"You know, I've seen his truck parked on the street for days, but I didn't think anything of it."

The news report showed a picture of the truck and

panned around our neighborhood. It made me proud to see our house in the background of one of the shots, and even if it was only being shown in connection to a murder that I had committed mostly in self-defense, it still made me proud to see it because it really was quite a nice neighborhood. I was also more thankful than ever that Donna's parents had lent us money for the down payment because otherwise we'd be living in a small condo or renting or possibly both.

A moment later, the detective whom I had met yesterday came up on the television screen, and he started saying that it was only a missing person case and that they were hopeful the man would be discovered unharmed. I felt that this was a bit naïve for him to say because I knew for a fact that Josh was about as far from unharmed as one could be, but then I figured maybe the detective was just an optimist, and there was no point faulting him for that, even if he was giving false hope to the community.

"I wonder if I should go talk to Hayley?" said Donna, after the news clip had ended. I suggested that perhaps it wouldn't be a good idea, but then Donna said she would go talk to her all the same, and so she put her shoes on and left me to look after Toby.

After locking the door behind her, I went into the kitchen where Josh's flowers were still prominently displayed on the kitchen counter. The "I love you" tag was still in the bouquet, and I wondered if I should remove it just in case someone recognized it and could identify the writing as his. Only then I wondered what would happen if Donna noticed the card was missing and started to ask a lot of questions, and if I answered them wrong then perhaps she would become suspicious of me and maybe even leave me and take Toby away with her. I was thinking about all of this when there came a knock at the door. I figured Donna must have forgotten something or needed some help, so I unlocked and opened the door only to discover the detective.

"Now there's a good mate, dinner all done and dusted?"

He was standing on the welcome mat on the front porch where Josh had smoked the cigar and made derogatory comments about marriage and the Morrison boy.

"Hello."

"Well, hello to you too, of course. Where are my manners to slip off like that? Yes. Hello, of course. And good evening."

By then, Molly had come up beside me and was wagging her tail and looking up at the detective. She seemed nearly ecstatic to see him, which I always found puzzling about dogs, since she'd never met him before and couldn't possibly know a thing about him. The way it was with dogs, it seemed that just about everyone who came to the door was the most wonderful and fascinating person they'd ever encountered. Sometimes I thought this made dogs naïve and even gullible, but then I thought that perhaps the opposite was true, and maybe most humans were just too suspicious and distrustful of one another, though I figured there was probably a happy balance between the two.

Then I started wondering if naïve and gullible basically meant the same thing, and I was wondering if I'd been redundant in my mind by using them both, but before I could think about it any further, the detective continued talking.

"Wonder if I could come in a spell, just to shake off the cobwebs?"

He was asking to come in, and though I certainly didn't want him to come inside, just as with Josh before I couldn't immediately think of a good excuse to say no, so instead I just opened the door, and he stepped into the foyer.

The cat had come out by then but remained back a fair distance. In this way, I found cats to be much more similar to humans than dogs because they seemed to have a healthy distrust of other people programmed into their DNA. It was this characteristic that I most respected about cats, only I also felt that cats took it too far because they acted the same way around people they'd known for years, and even people who were good to them and fed them and cleaned their litter boxes. So while I felt that cats were probably wiser than dogs in some ways, I also felt they were rather suspicious and ungrateful creatures.

"Mind if I keep my shoes on, mate?"

He didn't wait for me to answer before he stepped several feet inside.

"How may I help you?" I said.

"Straight to the point, then? That's a good, lad. That's a good fella."

He liked to refer to me in a number of different ways, and though at first I thought he might be mocking me by doing so, I later thought that maybe they just spoke differently where he was from, so I figured he probably didn't mean anything by it.

"I like to get right to the point too, you know. No need to drag things out any more than they need to. Always rub the missus the wrong way with the scenic route. Missus always tells me, get to the point and be done with it, isn't that right, mate? There's a good mate."

He was actually speaking to Molly when he said this. She'd come up to his side, and he'd knelt down and was now scratching behind her ears. By then she'd flopped over on her side, and I could see how happy she was with the detective, only I couldn't help wonder if she'd still be so pleased with him in that moment if she realized that he was surely only here to investigate me for the disappearance of Hayley's boyfriend. Only by the way her tongue was hanging out and the way that her legs were quivering, I suspected that she probably still would be.

"Well then, let's get right to it," he said, standing up. "I've now spoken with all of the immediate neighbors. All of them indeed. A fine set of neighbors you have here, that's what you've got, don't you, mate? Of course, you do. A right fine set of neighbors, indeed. There's a good mate with good neighbors."

"I suppose."

"And what I would do for neighbors like these," he said. "Always tell the missus that we need neighbors like these. That's what we need."

"They are all very pleasant," I said, "only sometimes the Morrison boy wears a helmet and a cape even when it's not Halloween, and some of the neighbors don't seem to like it."

"That a fact?"

"Yes," I said.

Toby would also wear a cape or a mask or other such things when it wasn't Halloween, only nobody seemed to care when he did it, and most people even felt it was cute, and they'd smile and some would even encourage him. Only most didn't find it cute when the Morrison boy did it, and though some of them would still smile, they were mostly strained smiles. The McGibbons were always very kind to the Morrison boy, however, unlike the acquisition of ceramic milk-dispensing cows, that behavior hadn't caught on quite the same way.

"Well then, about the neighbors. Talked to them all, one by one. Jolly hard work, I tell you. Jolly hard. And such fascinating stories they had to tell. Just fascinating. But I'm not telling you anything you don't know already, am I, mate?"

He called me mate an awful lot, which seemed to be something that he liked to do, though he used other names, too. Then I yawned because it had been a long day.

"I'm sorry, are you fagged?"

"No," I said.

"It's just you look a bit knackered, is all?"

Where I'd originally thought he was making a pejorative comment about my sexual orientation, it turned out that he was merely asking me if I was tired. I was then going to change my answer to "yes," only I didn't want to admit that I was so easily fooled, so I just repeated that I wasn't tired, even though I actually was.

"Back to it then," he said. "Now one of the neighbors, they recall seeing you leave in your vehicle on Saturday, just as you said, and right around the time your neighbor says that this young man came knocking about at your driveway. At least, that's the best that I can figure it."

"I suppose this is possible," I said.

"Bang to rights on that one, eh, fella?"

Much like when I thought he was asking me if I was a homosexual, I didn't understand what he'd just said. I was about to ask him to clarify, but then he started talking again before I had the chance.

"So it is possible then, isn't it, mate?"

"Yes," I said.

"Suppose you'd recollect where it was you buggered off to? Not trying to be too much a rozzer."

He used an awful lot of strange words, only I wondered if they sounded strange to him.

"Are you asking me where I went on Saturday?" I said.

"Quite right," he said, pointing and smiling just as he did when we first met, "that's just about the crux of the matter, Sonny Jim."

I presumed that all of that meant "yes"—but even if it didn't, I chose to answer it as if it did, so I explained to the detective that I'd gone for a ride because it was a beautiful sunny day and because Donna had taken Toby to a play date, and so I was by myself and had the time. By and large my account was an accurate one, even if I left out the part about stopping at the landfill to bury dismembered parts of Hayley's boyfriend.

"A ride then? Of course, charming area like this. A fine set of roads you've got to ride on, that's what you've got here, mate. A fine set of roads."

"Yes."

"And where was it you got off to?"

"No place in particular," I said.

"Oh, it was that kind of a drive, was it?" He chuckled, and I think I might even describe it as a hearty chuckle.

"Yes," I said.

At first, I wasn't sure if I should answer any of the

detective's questions because there was the chance I might accidentally incriminate myself in a way that I hadn't anticipated, but then I figured it was only guilty people who chose to remain silent, and even though I was, in fact, guilty, I didn't want to give the appearance of being guilty, so I figured I should try to answer his questions the best I could, and that if I left out the actual murder and indignity to the body then perhaps my answers might be good enough to satisfy him sufficiently to move onto another suspect. I also thought that if I was friendly to him and answered his questions quickly without actually confessing, then maybe he'd go away before Donna returned home, and that would probably save a lot of uncomfortable questions. The last time police had come calling on me and asking questions about a murder, it had upset Donna and perhaps had even shaken her belief in me as a person. I also remembered that she had briefly stopped helping me to achieve it, and even though this happened routinely since we'd started living together, I didn't want to make things any worse than they already were.

"Daddy, can I have some juice?"

Toby had just come out from the den. He was dragging a blanket behind him that he sometimes slept with during lightning storms and trauma naps. Both Donna and I had tried to wean him off the blanket because we felt he used it as an emotional crutch, but we'd also found that he'd wail and hyperventilate when we took it away, so we ultimately concluded that leaving it with him might be the lesser of two evils. I was also mindful of the article in the May issue of *The Child Psychology Magazine* "We Are Who We Are" and figured that maybe Toby just really liked blankets like some adults liked food or alcohol, so I decided not to be too fussed about it.

"Now look what we've got here," said the detective. "Now there's a good boy, there's a wee sunshine right there."

He was still talking nonsense, but I decided that this might be a perfect distraction, so I took Toby into the kitchen to get him some juice. Unfortunately, the detective followed right in after us.

"Nice kitchen you got here, mate." He was still wearing the same trench coat, and I could see sweat forming on his brow, but he didn't remove it.

"Can I get you a drink?" I asked after handing Toby his cup. I didn't actually want him to stay for a drink, but I figured that if I didn't at least offer him something then he might be more suspicious of me than he already was. Thankfully, he declined, which made me think he was just about ready to leave. That was when I looked up to see him staring at Josh's bouquet, which was still centered on the countertop.

"Very nice, mate. Very nice, indeed. Missus always on me to get her flowers."

He leaned in and smelled them.

"Donna enjoys flowers," I said. I said it because it was true.

"Lovely gesture. Lovely gesture, indeed, mate. There's a good mate, that's what you are, a good mate if I ever saw one." He drew back up and took stock around the kitchen, then said, "Don't suppose you thought of anything else, about that lazy Sunday drive, eh, Sonny Jim?"

"Saturday," I said.

The detective just smiled and said "Oh, yes, of course, how clumsy of me," but by the way he said it I could tell that it hadn't been a mistake at all, and that he was consciously trying to trick me with erroneous suggestions.

"So then," he continued, his eyes drawn back to and lingering on the flowers, "anything else, about that lazy Saturday drive?"

"No," I said.

"Maybe remember the path you took, now that you had time to think on it?"

"Not really," I said.

"You sure about that, mate?"

"Yes," I said.

"Well then, I suppose that's all I needed to hear. So sorry to bother you on this fine night. That's what you've got here, a fine night indeed."

I walked him to the foyer where he gave Molly another good scratch and then he finally opened the door to leave, but not before turning around at the last minute.

"Oh, chap, one last thing, if I might."

"Yes," I said.

"That ride you took, which you don't recall. Do you recall what time you left, exactly?"

"No," I said.

"Puzzling, puzzling."

He didn't seem particularly puzzled, and then soon enough he started talking again.

"And when you left, did you see our man Josh anywhere about?"

"No," I said.

"I see. Yes, of course you didn't, because you would have told me, old chap, wouldn't you? Would have told me straightway, knowing that I'm looking for the man? That's a good mate. That's what you are, is a good helpful mate if I've ever seen one."

"I suppose."

"Well then, I suppose that's all." He stepped out to the front porch, only then he stopped for a second time. "Oh, if I might ask, so sorry to be a bother, but if you would do me this smallest favor, being such a good chap as you are, and that's what you are—a good chap—if you could do me this smallest favor, and recall any of the streets that you drove through?"

"May I ask why you are asking me?" I said.

"Oh, now there I've gone and done it," he said.

"Gone and overstayed my welcome. Gone and offended you, haven't I, mate?"

"No," I said.

"Sure I have. And sure thing you want me to bugger off, that's what the missus says, that I always overstay my welcome, jabbering on about this and that. That's what the missus says, and she's a good missus if there ever was one."

I stared at him and he just kept talking.

"I apologize again, for being such a rozzer. Can't help myself, but the boy is missing, and his mother is worried. So I thought maybe you could help me, being perhaps the last man to see him, and being such a good mate as you are—that's what you are, of course, a good mate—that you could help me cover off some places that you were, if you didn't see him. Might help me to focus my search elsewhere, you see, if you could help me that much."

"I didn't pay all that much attention," I said.

"Right, mate, that's what you said before, I think, in not so many words. Tired of this old rozzer I'm sure, just like the missus. Don't mean to be a bother. Just an old bobbie trying to do his job. Lovely boy you have, and lucky missus you've got, with this home and those flowers. You've got it all, Sonny Jim, that's what you've got."

He didn't say anything more, just nodded to me one last time, and I finally closed the door behind him.

As soon as he was gone I walked directly to the

flowers, where I found the card almost precisely where he'd put his nose. I plucked it out and tore it up and buried it in the trash, which I figured would end up in the same landfill as Josh, and something about that seemed fitting.

Donna came home a while later and told me that Hayley was upset. Not only about Josh's disappearance but by the fact that the detective had been asking her many of the same types of questions that he had been asking me, and it occurred to me in that moment that despite his suspicions, he really had no idea what had happened to Josh, and I thought that maybe he was asking everyone the same questions he was asking me, and once again I became optimistic that it was the last I'd see of the detective. And even if this was gullible or naïve or possibly both if they meant the same thing, I felt optimistic all the same.

CHAPTER 18

At work the next day, I told Gordon about my visit with the detective. I wasn't sure why I brought it up exactly, since it had nothing to do with selling vacuums, except that I'd found that Gordon was easy to talk to, and even if we weren't all the way friends, I believed we were at least sufficiently friends to have the discussion.

"What are they talking to you for?"

"They believe that I may have been the last to see him alive," I said.

"Were you?"

I agreed that it was possible, even though it was more an outright certainty than a possibility, given that I'd stabbed him fourteen times with a carving knife I'd taken from the knife block. I told Gordon all that I knew about it, leaving out the actual murder, including the fight I'd heard the night before.

"Well, you better stop talking to them. Only reason they're talking to you is to pin it on you if they can."

"If I stop talking to them, they will think I am guilty."

"They don't care if you're guilty or not, they just want to clear the case off their books. Someone's gotta get charged."

"I see."

"Trust me, if this kid turns up dead, you better watch your ass."

"I suppose."

"I don't expect much from the police ever since what happened to my sister."

"You have a sister?" I said.

"I do."

"I see."

"That so surprising?"

"No," I said. The fact was that we'd hadn't spoken much about family, so I was surprised to hear that Gordon had a sister or a family of any sort. To me he was just Gordon.

"You think I ought to be off in a cave somewhere with my bat family, maybe?"

"No," I said. It seemed like Gordon might still be sore about the bat comment I'd made when I'd first met him, only then he went on talking as if he wasn't sore at all.

"Let me tell you about the police. My sister got car-jacked last year. Happened right in broad daylight in a parking lot. She looks up and sees a coffee shop, and there are a couple police cruisers out front. She runs up and starts banging on the window, and there's four of them sitting around a table with coffee and donuts."

"Did your sister get her car back?" I asked.

"You listening to me? That's not the fucking point. The point is people are getting jacked up and murdered out there, and the police are sitting on their asses drinking coffee and eating mother-fucking donuts. You think they're going to bust their ass finding the right person if you look ripe for the picking?"

The topic had clearly agitated Gordon, so I decided I should change the subject. I was just preparing to do so when Mr. Peters approached.

"Gentlemen."

"Afternoon, Frank."

I just nodded, because the last time I'd called him "Mr. Peters" in front of Gordon, it seemed to make him upset.

"So, will I see you both at the gallery on Friday?"

There was an annual art show sponsored by our company, and we were always given complimentary tick-ets. I'd never gone until I started dating Donna, but she usually wanted to go which meant that I was forced to attend in order to keep her happy and to increase the chances she would continue helping me to achieve it.

"You bet your ass," said Gordon, and I saw Mr. Peters smile when he said it, only it wasn't a full smile.

"I believe that Donna would like to attend," I said.

"I'm sure she does," said Peters, before adding, "It's the event of the season, after all."

I believe he overstated the situation, though given the fact that I wasn't familiar with many local events within the community, there was still the chance that he might have been telling the truth.

The art show brought a number of local artists together on the rooftop of a twenty-seven-story building. The president of our company apparently had a daughter who was a painter, and so he'd made the decision to host the event annually.

I remember wondering how much money it cost the company and how much more commission I might make on certain vacuums if they weren't paying for such an extravagant event, but then I also figured that I'd never know for sure, so there was no point dwelling on it, only then I'd dwelled on it anyway, and for some reason I came up with the figure of twenty-five cents more for each vacuum, which was a total guess but sounded about right in my head.

"You don't seem that excited," said Gordon, after Mr. Peters had finally walked away.

"Donna is looking forward to it," I said.

"Yeah, that's not what I said. I said *you* don't seem excited about it."

Gordon had a way of being direct with me that most people didn't. In some ways I respected him for this, but it also meant that most of the little tricks I'd learned to evade people didn't always work on him.

"I prefer to remain home most nights."

"Oh, yeah?"

"Yes."

"And why's that?"

I was going to tell him about how I found people difficult to talk to or generally disagreeable and how they always talked about things that were of no interest to me, only my parents had taught me that this was rude to say in so many words, so instead I just shrugged and changed the subject.

"Also, I don't believe the event is a wise expenditure."

"A wise expenditure?" said Gordon.

"Yes," I said.

"And why's that?"

"I believe they spend a lot of money on the event, and it's money that could be used in the commission of our vacuums."

"You figure?"

"Yes."

"You're a strange cat," he said. Gordon was not the first to point out that I was different, but he at least said it in a way that suggested he was not being cruel or de-meaning. "This shindig open bar?"

"Yes."

"Then I'm going to give myself a raise," he said.

This was Gordon's way of saying that he was going to drink a lot of alcohol on the company's tab. There were times in the past that I would also consume a lot of alcohol, only it interfered with my impulse control, so I tried to limit my alcohol consumption whenever possible, and while I'd found there was a direct correlation between the amount of alcohol consumed by myself and Donna with the number of times she would help me to achieve it, I'd also found there was a direct correlation between my alcohol consumption and the number of times I would want to make people red and open, so I figured it was better that I achieve it less often with Donna if it meant less chance of committing cold-blooded murder.

"I'm sorry to hear about your sister," I said.

He looked at me when I said it, but it wasn't the same incredulous, disdainful look that he often used, so I felt that perhaps our friendship was developing after all.

"You just stop talking to that detective."

I nodded.

"You promise?"

"Yes," I said.

Then Gordon turned back to his computer, and alt-hough it seemed as if he'd moved on from our conversation and was ready to commit to his work, I could tell that he hadn't moved on all the way because he was shaking his head and kept mumbling "Coffee and fucking do-nuts."

CHAPTER 19

The next day at work, I received a phone call from Toby's school.

It was Miss Mullen on the phone and she asked me if I could come in, and I asked her if Toby was all right, and she said that he was, except she also said that there'd been "an incident," which I understood was just a euphemism for saying that something terrible had happened, such as when I'd stabbed Molly's original owner seventeen times in the neck with my Swiss Army knife with the polar bear handle.

"Incident?' I said.

I was hoping that Toby hadn't done anything particularly violent or anti-social because then we'd surely have to "Find His Freud" and try to correct his behavior, assuming it wasn't already too late. My own parents had often tried to find me the right psychiatrist, psychologist, or otherwise educated person, and though it fixed me in some ways, it clearly didn't fix me all the way.

"I'm afraid Toby pushed Timmy off of his chair."

This made me think of the time that I was sent to the principal because I'd pushed Sally Tannenbaum off her chair for saying that dogs were stupid animals, though I suppose it might have just ended there had I not picked up my compass and tried to do what I did with it.

"And then he kicked him," added Miss Mullen.

"I see."

"In the head," she added.

This all seemed very serious. Then I said so.

"It is serious," said Miss Mullen. "Could you possibly come to the school?"

"Have you called Donna?" I asked. It wasn't that I didn't care about my son, but the fact was that I felt Donna was better equipped to handle social interactions than I was.

"Yes, we called her first, but there was no answer, so I left her a message. Do you think you could possibly come?"

I agreed to come and then hung up the telephone.

As I stood up Gordon asked me if anything was wrong, so I told him there'd been an incident at Toby's school. Then he asked me what kind of incident, which was a fair question, so I answered it, though I suppose I would have done so even if it had been an unfair question.

"You better get over there, then."

It wasn't much of a suggestion because it was obvious I was on my way, and because he'd probably even heard me tell Miss Mullen that I was on my way, but I suppose he just meant to be supportive.

I went to Mr. Peters' office and told him I had to leave and explained the situation, and he clapped me on my shoulder and said "Better go see about your boy," so I nodded to him and left.

As I arrived at the school, I saw a number of kids running wildly outside and it appeared as if they were all trying to make each other red and open, only then as I got closer, it became clear that they were simply outside for recess and they were roughhousing as children were wont to do, and which was why I mostly kept to myself during recess when I was a boy. I stepped inside the school and found Toby seated in the waiting area of the office.

"Hello," I said.

Toby just hung his head down even lower than it had already been.

"I was called by Miss Mullen."

He remained silent.

"She says that you kicked Timmy."

Still he didn't answer.

"I'm afraid that you will have to answer these questions," I said.

Before he could respond, I saw the principal walking forward. He greeted me with a hearty handshake and invited me into his office. He also asked for Toby to remain outside so that we could speak "privately," which was something that used to happen to me with my own parents.

"Please have a seat," he said.

He extended his hand toward one of the chairs, which seemed entirely unnecessary because it would have been awfully strange if I'd chosen to sit on his desk or the floor or even the windowsill, where he had a small cactus.

Only then I couldn't help wondering if maybe in the past he'd invited someone to sit down in his office, and they had actually sat down on his desk or the floor or the windowsill by the cactus, which would perhaps have explained why he was being so cautious.

"Well then, about this unpleasantness."

"Yes."

"It would seem that the relationship between Toby and Timothy has begun to deteriorate."

"It would appear so," I said.

"It is troubling," he said. "We had seen such an improvement in the last week."

"Yes," I said.

"Unfortunately, neither boy has spoken about what precipitated the disagreement."

I wondered if he'd actually used the word "precipitated" when discussing the matter with the children, which might explain why they didn't answer.

"Toby is sometimes quiet," I said.

"He certainly is."

"Many children are not quiet."

"No, I suppose not."

"I saw many boys and girls outside, and they do not seem reluctant to speak because I could hear them screaming when I walked in. Perhaps one of these children might provide a witness statement."

"Well, this isn't exactly a criminal investigation."

"No," I said, "but I suppose one of them still might wish to provide a statement, if given the opportunity."

The principal just looked at me curiously. Then he said, "We prefer to speak directly to the affected parties."

"A witness statement from one of the other children might be even better, as it would be received without bias."

In my law class in college, we were taught about the value of witness statements, particularly from independent witnesses who had no perceived motive for fabricating their evidence. Only then I thought that perhaps some of the screaming children might be friends with Toby or Timmy and how their responses might be biased after all, and that perhaps some of the children might even collude in their responses, so I told the principal that if he did seek independent statements, he ought to be careful to safeguard against bias or collusion.

"These are four-year-old children," said the principal.

"Of course," I said.

He straightened up in his chair, which was something that I found people did when they felt uncomfortable or wanted to change the subject, though I suppose it could have been both. "Although we do not know the source of the disagreement," he said, "we are aware of the physical interaction that occurred between the two boys."

"Miss Mullen told me what happened," I said. "Is the boy okay?"

"He will be fine. His mother already came to take him home."

"I see."

"Yes, well, you can imagine that this is quite concerning. Our school has a zero tolerance policy for violence."

"I do not believe this is entirely accurate," I said.

This seemed to frustrate the principal because he started to fidget behind his desk. Only I couldn't help thinking about how Timmy had punched Toby in the eye and was allowed to remain enrolled in the class, so I concluded that the principal was exaggerating the school's zero tolerance policy for violence, and I concluded that they must at least have "some tolerance" for violence. Then I said so.

"No, sir, we do not have some tolerance for violence," he said.

"Then I believe you are not applying the policy equally," I said.

Again, he fidgeted behind his desk.

"Will Toby be suspended?" I said.

He leaned back in his chair and crinkled his brow when I said it.

"These are four-year-olds," he said, only this didn't answer the question, and after a moment of me continuing to look at him he continued, "We don't suspend four-year-olds, you see? They wouldn't appreciate the deterrent implications of that action. We don't suspend kids from school until at least middle school."

"I see," I said, only I knew this wasn't completely true, because I remembered having been suspended at least once before middle school, only in that case I hadn't kicked a boy in the head so much as I'd thrown a rock at someone's head, and the boy had ended up bloody and crying, and I remember how he'd run to the teacher in tears, and when my parents came to pick me up from the principal's office and asked me what I'd done, I'd explained to them quite truthfully that the boy was throwing rocks at seagulls, and so it only seemed fair that I throw rocks at him in return. That was the first time my father told me that "Winners don't throw rocks," which was his way of saying that successful people don't resort to violence to settle their issues. Going forward, anytime I did something violent or physical to another person he would always say, "Winners don't throw rocks," even if the weapon in that case wasn't a rock at all but a pen or a pencil or a compass, and even if I wasn't so much throwing those things as much as I was stabbing those things into people's necks, legs, or eyes.

"So, what do you think?"

When I finally came out of my remembering, it occurred to me that the principal had been speaking the entire time, only my thoughts had been so loud they were the only things I could hear. "Perhaps this is an opportunity to try a different action plan," I said, even though I had no frame of reference for what to say because I hadn't heard a word he'd just said.

The principal just looked at me when I said it as if perhaps he thought I was mocking him, which was not the case at all. The fact was that I very much hoped that the school's strategies would be successful, because if you couldn't even spit into the wind without it costing you money, I could only imagine how much it would cost to pay for a psychiatrist, psychologist, or otherwise educated person. Finally, he cleared his throat and said, "I'm glad you are willing to work with us on a solution."

"Of course," I said.

He was still eyeing me curiously as I stood up and told him that I was going to take Toby home, and when he didn't say anything further, I figured it was okay to leave, and so I did.

එංඑං

We arrived home to discover that Josh's truck was gone, and since I knew that Josh himself was in no condition to move it, I figured that it must have been driven away by the police, or his mother, or perhaps even towed away by the city. But whichever the case, I was relieved that it was no longer parked on our street because it had served as a daily reminder of what I'd done.

Once inside, I thought that it would be a good idea if Toby had some rest, so I tucked him into bed and started to move away, only before I could get all the way out the door he asked me to tell him a story. As usual, I told him that Mommy was best at telling stories and somehow managed to placate him in some other way, and soon enough he fell asleep. It was obvious that Toby was fatigued because he didn't put up much of a fight, and he even fell asleep right in the middle of our conversation, and while I figured this might have been one of his exhaustion naps, I wasn't sufficiently convinced to place it firmly in this category, so I left it unlabeled in my mind, which was rare because my mind was usually able to fill in the gaps.

After Donna got home, we discussed what to do with Toby.

"What did they expect him to do, getting bullied the way he has been?"

I didn't say anything, so she kept talking.

"When you think about it that way, he was really just acting in self-defense."

Donna tended to side with Toby no matter what he did, which in one way showed unwavering support, but in another way might serve to hinder his appreciation of what is right and what is wrong.

"The principal believes his actions were excessive," I said.

While I may not have been in the best position to speak to what was a sufficient response in a self-defense situation, I couldn't help but think that kicking someone in the face when they were in a prone position on the floor exceeded the scope of acceptable retaliation.

"I just think that if they can't supervise the kids properly, then it's good that he can defend himself, that's all."

"We do not know for sure that it was self-defense," I said.

This seemed to resonate with Donna because she suddenly became very quiet, which was rare.

"It would appear that Toby is too young to be suspended," I said.

"I'd certainly hope so," she said.

"You do not need to hope. The principal told me himself."

Donna giggled when I said this. She often found the things I said and did to be amusing, and this seemed to be another one of those times.

Following dinner, we finally got Toby to discuss the incident. He told us that it had occurred during lunchtime, and that he was preparing to eat his dessert when Timmy approached him and asked to have it, but unlike the time with the Spiderman chocolates, he only had the one, so he declined, but then Timmy tried to take it from him by force, and then what happened had happened.

Hearing this explanation, I was much less concerned than I had been before, and I figured that Toby might have even been justified in responding the way that he had. I'd learned in my law class that people could use reasonable force in defense of their property, and although our law professor didn't expand on the parameters of what you could defend, I figured that even a chocolate chip muffin with cream cheese frosting would probably qualify.

CHAPTER 20

We dropped Toby off at school the next day in a show of family support. After taking him inside, we were walking back to the car when I saw Timmy's father approaching us quickly from the sidewalk.

"You and I need to talk," he said, pointing at me as he did.

"You wish to talk about the incident between our boys?" I said.

"You bet your ass," he said, and I could tell by the tone of his voice that he was angry.

I asked him what he would like to discuss, and he said that he had a problem with what Toby had done yesterday, only he didn't use those exact words, and the words that he did use were filled with profanity.

The moment made me think of the Blackhawk Down article in that month's issue of *The Child Psychology Magazine*, because it was clear that Timmy's father was upset about how his son had been treated and was now reacting in an overprotective manner much as Donna had when I first told her that Toby was being bullied. I was going to take the opportunity to share some of the lessons from Blackhawk Down, only I couldn't help but think about how the last time I'd tried implementing a child psychology technique with an adult it had ended with me driving out to the landfill while forgetting my dog outside in the backyard. There was obviously more to it than just that, but sometimes I liked to gloss over the bad parts, even in my own mind.

"Anyone messing with my son's gonna get a shit-kickin.'"

I could see his nostrils flaring as he said it.

By then I was thinking about how he seemed much more concerned about the physical interaction between the children now than he had been when we'd first met. Then I said it.

"Oh, being a smartass, huh?"

"No," I said, though I did see how he might have thought so.

"Our son didn't start this," said Donna.

I saw his face go even redder when she said it, only I wasn't sure if it was what she'd said or who had said it that upset him. "I believe the force he used to defend his property was at least sufficiently reasonable, even if it wasn't all the way reasonable."

Timmy's father looked at me queerly after I said it.

"Plus," I said, "Timmy had been bullying Toby, and this can be traumatic for some children. There was an article in the June issue of *The Child Psychology Magazine*. Have you read it?"

He looked as confused as he was angry.

"The article was called 'Bullying Is The New Purple,'" I said.

It seemed clear from his reaction that not only hadn't he read it, but that something about the mention of it made him even angrier because he looked at me as if he wanted to make me red and open, and I could even see that his hands were clenched like maybe he was going to hit me, and I thought about how it would be ironic if he struck me so soon after we'd been talking about fighting and bullying. Only he didn't hit me after all, but he did call me a "fucking weirdo."

Then Donna said "Whoa, whoa," and I thought that maybe she was trying to de-escalate the situation, since that was the same sort of calming language that people sometimes used on riled up horses just before they'd give a warm rub to the side of the horse's head or even offer them a sugar cube, only then she added, "better a weirdo than a degenerate," and this seemed very much like an escalation.

That's when I saw the principal approaching.

"Is there a problem here?"

None of us said anything, which would have made for an awkward scene had I not much preferred the silence.

Finally, Timmy's father pointed his finger in my direction and said, "You don't want to see me again," and while I believe he meant this to be menacing, it was also an entirely accurate statement, so I couldn't help but agree.

We spoke briefly with the principal about what had happened, but decided to leave it at that. Donna and I then spoke in the parking lot, and she told me that Timmy's father was more concerned with his own ego than he was with his son's welfare, and that she believed the matter was now personal to him, and that I needed to "watch myself"—and though Donna surely didn't mean it to be menacing, I couldn't help but feel some small sense of trepidation as a result.

☙❧☙

Later that night, I saw a news bulletin on the television, and it had a picture of Josh and some basic biographical data and information pertaining to his last known whereabouts. It said that the police suspected foul play in his disappearance and included a phone number at the bottom of the screen where people could phone in with any confidential tips or information. But what was even more interesting was that the news report included someone who claimed to have seen him only yesterday. There was a horse track in the next town, and the person said that they saw him standing near the horse paddock before one of the races. I knew this was impossible because Josh was in no position to be standing anywhere yesterday, let alone betting on horses, however I couldn't help but think how this might satisfy the police that he was indeed still alive, and that maybe soon enough the entire matter would be forgotten.

CHAPTER 21

Friday night Donna and I went to the rooftop art gala.

We'd dropped Toby off at Donna's parents' home for the night, which meant that we could stay out as late as we wanted and drink alcohol, and I figured that Donna would probably help me to achieve it later, even if this wasn't a sure thing anymore since we'd started living together.

Since Donna and I both worked for the same company, there were lots of people we both knew. I introduced her to Gordon, who was walking with a cane and had on dark sunglasses even though we were outside and the sun had gone down nearly two hours ago. Gordon often wore sunglasses whether it was day or night out, which was something that a lot of blind people liked to do.

There must have been two hundred people up on the roof looking at the different pieces of art, most of which were set up beneath large umbrellas or canopies in the event of rain. There were also caterers walking around with hors d'oeuvre and champagne, and even if they didn't actually call them hors d'oeuvre anymore, that's what they were to me.

"What do you think of this one?"

Donna was looking at a piece of art that showed a person's face, except the nose and the eyes had switched spots. The artist was standing beside it and she was a young woman with long dark hair who happened to have her own nose and eyes in the right places.

"What does it mean?" I said.

The artist smiled at me and said that it epitomized confusion, only when I asked her what was so confusing about it she didn't have much to say. That's when I saw the price tag, which to me seemed like the most confusing part of all. Donna and I never actually bought any of the art pieces because they were all so expensive and because money was usually tight after we'd paid all of our monthly bills. It didn't help that Donna liked to go to the stores and purchase shoes and makeup, and though I felt she probably had more shoes than anyone could possibly need, she always managed to come back with more. One time I even told her that I thought she had enough shoes and perhaps should stop buying new pairs, and she became very quiet as women sometimes do, and as Toby sometimes does when we won't buy him a new toy. I found that women and children could behave very similarly in similar circumstances, but I only said this sort of thing in my head, because the one time I said it with my mouth Donna stopped helping me to achieve it for nearly two weeks.

Donna told the artist "we'll think about it," which was what people said to be nice when they didn't want to buy something and just wanted to escape from the situation. We were taught different ways to overcome this at my company, which usually involved psychological tricks that created a heightened sense of urgency. Our company was always teaching us new ways to tap into the vulnerabilities of our customers and to foster urgency, even though the only real urgency seemed to be related to their profits.

Donna then saw somebody that she used to work with, and she waved and told me she was going to go talk to her. She asked if I would be okay on my own, and while the fact was that being on my own was not only bearable but was actually preferable, this type of truthful answer was usually received in much the same way as suggestions about her shoe purchases, so I instead just said "I will be okay," which also happened to be true.

I took the opportunity to move to a quiet spot in the far corner. We were up twenty-seven floors, and while I didn't particularly like heights, I took the opportunity to

look out over the edge at all the little people walking
down below. I wasn't there long before I heard a voice
call my name, and I turned around to see Gordon.

"I thought that was you," he said, then added, once
he was closer, "you see the prices on this shit?"

"Yes," I said.

"Starving artists, my ass."

It was true that none of them looked like they were
starving, only then I wasn't thinking about how much the
artists ate as much as I was wondering how Gordon could
even see any of the art, or find me for that matter. As it
turned out, he had some special monocle he could hold
up to his one eye that he could look into that helped him
make out certain shapes and images as long as the detail
wasn't too fine.

"Did you see the one with the mixed-up face?" I
said.

"Two thousand dollars!" said Gordon. He seemed to
scoff when he said it.

"It epitomizes confusion," I said.

"Yeah, it epitomizes something, all right."

Gordon was what our boss Mr. Peters might consider
"a challenger." This was someone who took a contrarian
position to most things. This was the opposite of a "yes
man," which companies seemed to prefer. It made me
wonder why they'd hired Gordon in the first place, only I
figured maybe contrarians were slightly less so during the
interview process.

We continued talking, just the two of us, when all of a sudden I heard a loud voice from the crowd.

"Now there's Sonny Jim, that's who we've got there, gawd blimey, that's Sonny Jim, all right."

I looked up to see the detective appear through the crowd. He walked right up to where we were standing and extended his hand in my direction. I wasn't sure what to do because his appearance was so unexpected, and I immediately thought that maybe this was a police trick like when we would ask our customers if they'd like us to check to see if a particular vacuum was in stock even though we'd just checked five minutes ago and there were two hundred. Our company told us this wasn't a lie or dishonest at all because we could offer to check the stock of our products as often as we wanted to, and if the customer decided to extrapolate this into meaning the product was in short supply, then that was their business. Mr. Peters once overheard me tell a customer that we had 187 left in the warehouse, and he told me that we shouldn't be disclosing that sort of information because it decreased the sense of urgency. This was what the company referred to as a "coaching moment." Just as the company used the word opportunity in place of problem, they also liked to use the word "coaching" when what was actually happening was a lecture or possibly even punishment. I felt that these sales tactics ran afoul of the company culture to "assault them with honesty"—but I'd complied for fear of getting fired, and while I doubt that the detective was trying to create a false sense of urgency by offering his hand, there was always the possibility he was trying to gather evidence, such as obtaining a sample of my DNA or maybe even to test my strength to better gauge the likelihood I could have subdued Hayley's boyfriend. And though I didn't want to give the detective an investigative edge that he didn't previously possess, I figured that it was only guilty people who didn't shake police officers' hands when offered. Only then I thought that there were probably a lot of people who might not want to shake a police officer's hand, such as people with a phobia of germs, or Gordon's people, or any other people who might have a healthy distrust of law enforcement.

I finally decided that I would shake his hand, but just as I was about to extend mine, he finally withdrew his own, perhaps because it was taking me so long to decide. This made me think about how often my thinking was unnecessary and went nowhere, and I couldn't help but laugh at how absurd it all was.

"Is something funny, mate?"

I thought about relaying the substance of the conversation that I'd just had in my mind, but then I'd found that the words in my head often didn't translate well in real life, and that things that I found to be funny or amusing in my head sometimes came across as bizarre or puzzling to others based on the looks on some people's faces, so instead I just said that I was thinking of something funny, which was a simpler answer, and one that also happened to be true.

"Yes, I see," said the detective. "A good jovial chap, that's what we've got here then, a good jovial chap. There's a good chap."

I didn't respond to that because I didn't know how. That's when the detective seemed to notice Gordon.

"And who have we got here, mate?"

I introduced Gordon to the detective, and while the detective immediately said it was "a pleasure," I could tell by the look on Gordon's face that he didn't feel the same way in return.

"Why have you come here?" I asked.

"Oh, and there I've gone and done it again. Missus always tells me the same thing, about dropping in on people. That's what the missus tells me."

"Have you been following me?" I asked.

"This is harassment," added Gordon, before he could respond.

"Oh my," said the detective. "Never thought of it like that, never thought of it like that at all, mate, this a public event and all. They're selling tickets you know, down-stairs in the lobby. Bought one myself, being a fan of art and all that, thought I might take a butcher's." He paused long enough to reach into his pocket and pull out his tick-et, "And if you happen to be here, then all the better. Two birds and one stone sort of thing. Just to be efficient.

Can't blame an old bobbie for trying to be efficient, can you, mate?"

"I do not believe you are here to see the art," I said, and the detective began to chuckle.

"Well now, there's a clever mate, quick as ever." He pointed at me with his ticket as he said it. "Saw right through it, did you, mate? There's a good clever mate if I ever saw one. Sharp as a tack, this one. Mickey the dunce need not apply here, eh, mate? There's a good Sonny Jim."

I didn't particularly understand what he'd just said, but it seemed that he was agreeing with me as best I could tell.

"Then best I get right to the point, so as not to interfere with your evening any more than I already have. What say you to that, mate? Shall we get straightaway to the point? That's what the missus always tells me, to get right to the point, that's what she tells me."

"Why don't you just spit it out?" said Gordon.

The detective looked down at Gordon, then he softened his voice a bit, into something just above a whisper. "Well now, delicate subject such as this, I wonder if you might wish to talk somewhere more private."

Just like not wanting to shake his hand, I felt it was only guilty people who wanted to talk in private, so I told the detective that anything he had to say to me, he could say in front of Gordon, and so he did.

"Well then, funny thing, you see. Did a little check,

mate. Just looking into the history of old Sonny Jim, here. Turns out you've had a previous brush with the bobbies, isn't that right, mate?"

"Yes," I said.

I knew what he was referring to, which was the police investigation from five years ago when I'd been investigated for the disappearance of my landlord and also the murder of a man named Sherman Dempsey in an alleyway. I didn't much want Gordon hearing these things, but then I figured nothing could be done about it at this point. I was also distracted by the fact he'd just said "check mate," and I was wondering if he'd thought about chess when he said it just as I had. Sometimes my brain would wander to small insignificant things such as that, and even if the thought didn't mean anything, I still had to deal with it once it was there, and this was another one of those times.

"Got yourself into a good bit of Barney Rubble there, didn't you, mate?"

Again I didn't understand what that meant, but as was the case with most people, if you didn't say anything, they would usually just keep on talking. Most people enjoyed talking an awfully lot, which worked out well for people like me who didn't much like talking, at least not with actual words.

"Called up the inspector, I did. Had a good chat about one Sonny Jim, that's what we did. Turns out the charges didn't stick. Seems like you took the Mick on that one, didn't you, mate? There's a good mate, taking the Mick. That's what you are, of course, a good mate."

I couldn't imagine he really thought of me as a good mate since he clearly suspected me of foul play in the disappearance of Hayley's boyfriend, so I felt that by saying so he was being rather patronizing. Only then I remembered that he was from England and how they talked funny, and how maybe it was just a common turn of phrase, so I decided not to be too fussed about it.

"I was cleared of those charges," I said.

"Cleared you say? Bollocks. You were only a suspect in the investigation. There were no charges laid, eh, mate? Hard to be cleared of charges that don't get laid, eh, Sonny Jim?" He was still speaking in a jovial tone of voice even though he wasn't being very friendly.

"Look, you going to charge my friend or just keep talking?" said Gordon.

"Oh, charges, you say? Back we are talking about charges, are we? Surely hadn't thought about that. Unless, of course, you believe that you should be charged. And what say you, Sonny Jim?"

It was clear that the detective was fishing for more evidence. This was similar to what the inspector had done when he'd had suspicions about me but didn't have enough evidence to charge me. It was clear that the detective was trying to get me to do or say something incriminating, and showing up to my work function was surely a police tactic that might exacerbate my reaction, and while this might be good police work, I couldn't help but think of the embarrassment this might cause me with some of my friends and colleagues. I was also worried that Donna would see, and I instinctively glanced over the ledge of the building and couldn't help but wonder what it might be like if the detective fell over the edge, and how maybe that would resolve all of this, and things could go on back to how they were before.

"Well then," repeated the detective, "what say you?"

"I saw on television that someone saw him standing near the horse paddock."

"Yes, right you are, quick as a fiddle this one," and again he pointed at me with his ticket.

"Perhaps you should speak to the witness."

"Oh, we certainly did. A nutter, of course. A gambler and a degenerate. You know the type, don't you, mate?"

"No," I said.

He was dismissing the man as a kook, only I remember how my father used to say that "sometimes even the kooks have it right." And even though I knew this particular kook was not right, I also knew that the detective couldn't be certain of it.

"Of course not," he said, then began to laugh a deep and hearty laugh, as if what I'd said was incredibly funny. It caused a number of nearby people to look over.

"I would prefer if you would leave," I said.

"Yes, no doubt you would. Can't be much fun with the bobbies up here, talking about such unpleasant things.

What with your missus here, too, of course. And what would she think of all this, what indeed?"

He glanced over his shoulder as if he was looking for Donna. This was the detective's way of intimating that he knew that she was here and that he could make things uncomfortable for me.

"I do not wish you to bother Donna," I said, and I could feel myself getting angry.

"Yes, Donna, is it? The missus says I need to be better with names, that's what the missus says. Donna, you say? Yes, I promise not to forget that. Won't forget that again, old chap."

Again, he turned to look into the crowd in order to telegraph to me that he was looking for Donna, and while I felt that I'd maintained my composure fairly well to that point, now I could feel my fingernails digging into the underside of my clenched palms, and I could feel the temperature on my forehead and neck growing red and hot.

Gordon started talking to the detective, and I could see him speaking back to Gordon, and the detective's mouth was moving and he was smiling as he spoke, and I focused right on his lips that kept talking and talking, only by then everything was in slow motion. Then he turned back in my direction and said something to me that I didn't even hear, and rather than asking him to repeat it, I just grabbed the detective by the lapels of his jacket and drove him forward over the side of the building, then looked over the edge of the roof and watched as he plummeted down to the earth frantically waving his arms and legs as he fell, and as I watched his body explode on the pavement, I could only think that in those last few seconds of life he must have been thinking I was not such a good mate after all, and perhaps was even re-evaluating his original choice to come up here, if his brain worked fast enough to do so before it detonated from the impact.

"What happened?" asked Gordon. "What was that scream?"

I didn't answer him because I'd noticed how everyone on the roof had turned deathly silent and they were now staring at me with their mouths gaping, and I saw the young artist and figured she'd probably be the first to admit that this epitomized confusion more than her painting ever could, and I looked through the crowd to see Donna staring back at me in horror, and then everyone started screaming and running from the roof, and I ran along with them, shoving people aside in a frantic scramble to escape the murder scene. And as I ran down the stairs pushing my way past the people, I was already thinking about how I could get past security and from the building to the nearest bank where I would withdraw what meager resources I had, and how I'd have to live on the run as a fugitive and how I probably wouldn't make it very far unless I was more resourceful than I thought.

"You feeling all right, mate?"

This was the detective speaking to me. Just as with

Timmy's father at the school, I had only committed the murder in my mind. But I admit that it felt good to think it, and by thinking through to the logical consequences of my actions, it helped me to simmer down enough to hear their voices again.

"Why don't you go talk to the woman?" said Gordon.

"The woman?" said the detective.

"Yeah, the partner. Why are you harassing this man? This stuff is always domestic, isn't it? Why aren't you shaking her down?" Then Gordon turned to me and said, "Tell him."

This comment seemed to pique the detective's interest.

"Tell me what, mate?"

"He told me everything," said Gordon. "Woke up the night before this dude went missing to a hell of a fight next door. Heard crashing and breaking. Isn't that right?"

"Is this true?" said the detective before I had a chance to answer Gordon. He seemed very serious for the first time that night.

"Yes," I said.

"And might you explain, good sir, why you never told me this before?"

"I didn't think much of it," I said, and that was the truth.

"Now maybe you can stop harassing good people, and go and do some actual police work," said Gordon.

"And you say this was the night before he went missing?"

"Yes," I said.

He took out his police notebook for the first time that night and scribbled down some additional details.

"And what was it exactly that you heard and saw?"

I explained it all as best I could, and the detective scribbled everything down in his notebook.

"I thank you, sir. That will be all for now." Then he immediately left.

I was grateful to Gordon, who had seemingly thrown him off the trail, and while I felt bad that this might cast suspicion on Hayley, the fact was that I knew Hayley was innocent, so I figured nothing more would come of it.

ოთხ

Donna and I returned home later that night, and she was clearly in a good mood from all the champagne, and I could tell that she wanted to help me achieve it, so I went upstairs to take a quick shower. She briefly came into the bathroom as I did and we talked about this or that, and I tried to finish up as quickly as I could to join her in the bedroom. Unfortunately, she was in a very different mood by the time I got there, so instead I just watched some television and went to sleep, but all in all I still felt it was a successful night, all things considered.

CHAPTER 22

Donna behaved similarly in the morning, which was to say she was acting quiet and distant as women sometimes do when they are upset and either unable or unwilling to articulate what is bothering them, so I decided not to press her on the matter and instead just kissed her on the cheek and went to work, where I had a largely uneventful day and sold four vacuums.

I arrived home just after five and found Hayley outside in her front yard with an odd look on her face.

"Good afternoon," I said.

She walked in my direction very slowly, and I could see that her face had lost most of its color.

"The police were here today," she said.

I didn't say anything, so she continued.

"They were here for hours. I had to come home from work to let them in. They had a warrant to search my home."

"I see."

"They say they have reason to believe that I was involved in Josh's disappearance."

"You have already told them all that you know," I said.

"Yes, but they don't seem to believe me."

I could see that her hands were trembling, and I knew that what Gordon had said yesterday must have been the basis of their getting a warrant and searching Hayley's home, and while I felt a certain level of guilt for this, I also knew full well that there was nothing to find as I had committed the murder in my own home and buried Josh's body well away from here, so I tried to calm her down and ease her mind because I knew she was innocent and had done nothing wrong.

"I know that," she said, "but they don't seem to."

"Perhaps they are just being thorough."

"Perhaps."

"Also," I added, "I heard that someone saw him walking near the horse paddock," and though I knew the person who said this was incorrect, the fact remained that I had indeed heard the rumor spoken, so repeating that I'd heard it wasn't actually a lie. In fact, many people in the neighborhood were discussing it, and there was even a rumor circling around that he might have gotten himself into debt with the wrong people and run off or been killed as a result.

"I heard that too. Only I never knew Josh to gamble."

"I see."

I was trying to think of some other comforting thing to say, but before anything came to mind, I saw Donna pulling into the driveway with Toby. Donna eyed us curiously as she stepped from the car before retrieving Toby from the booster seat.

"Daddy," he said, running up to me and grabbing ahold of my leg.

Hayley remained standing with her arms crossed tightly around her chest as if she were cold.

I asked Toby how school was and he said "Fine," which for children of Toby's age usually meant precisely that. Then I asked Donna how her day was, and she also said "Fine," which I'd come to learn could have meant any number of things.

"What's going on?" said Donna.

"The police came to Hayley's home today. It seems they had a search warrant."

"Really?" said Donna.

Hayley nodded but didn't say anything.

"Well, I'm sure they just have to do that," said Donna, "to be thorough."

Again, Hayley nodded, only this time not as forcefully, and then a moment later she began to cry. Donna then moved in to give her a hug and told her that things would be all right.

I was going to say something supportive as well, but I always found it difficult to talk to crying women, so instead all I said was "Say hello to Mister Muggles," which may not have been the most comforting thing to say in that situation, but it was the first thing that came to mind and the best I could offer under the circumstances.

Donna took Hayley back inside her house, so I brought Toby inside where he immediately started playing with some Lego. This gave me the opportunity to let Molly into the backyard and go upstairs to change out of my work clothes and take a shower. I'd been daily applying cover up to the marks that Josh had left around my neck, and I did so once again before Donna could return, which she did about thirty minutes later. Then we all had dinner around the kitchen table while Molly laid down beside us and chewed on her bone, and I couldn't help thinking how it was very much a traditional family moment, much like a Norman Rockwell painting, except for the part about my neighbor being investigated for a murder that I'd committed.

"How is Hayley?" I asked.

"She is beside herself," said Donna.

"Did the police find anything?" I asked.

"She says she doesn't know. They wouldn't let her in the house while the search was occurring."

"I see."

"But she says there were a number of officers, and some of them left carrying items in plastic baggies."

I'd learned from a law class in college that police would sometimes get a search warrant when they had reasonable grounds to believe that a crime had been committed, and they would take pictures and swab different surfaces when they saw stains, and then those swabs would be tested by a scientist, and while they sometimes came back as blood or saliva or some other meaningful bodily substance, they would just as often come back as Aunt Jemima or Mrs. Butterworth's or possibly some other brand of syrup that I'd never even heard of.

"She says that she's going to consult a lawyer," said Donna.

"I suppose that's reasonable."

Our professor had also taught us that if you were charged with an offence that it was a good idea to consult a criminal defense lawyer early in the process, and that there were many different tricks and strategies the lawyers could use to help a guilty person escape liability, so I figured it was probably a good idea for Hayley to consult one, because if lawyers could be that effective with people who were guilty, I could only imagine what they could do for an actually innocent person.

After dinner, we had brownies for dessert, and Toby bit into his and made a growling sound like a dog as he did, and while I initially thought that maybe he was trying to communicate with Molly, I then noticed Molly wasn't even in the room. Then Toby disclosed to us that he'd bitten Timmy that day during recess. Donna set her fork down on her plate, presumably to highlight the solemnity of the moment, though it's possible she was just full, or perhaps felt it was heavy. Then she asked Toby if he was telling the truth, and he nodded before again biting into the brownie and making more dog noises.

I couldn't be sure that Toby was telling the truth, given that we hadn't heard anything about this from the school, and while I generally found my son to be honest and trustworthy, the fact remained that he was only four years old, and given that he sometimes still defecated in his pants, I felt this also detracted from his credibility.

Donna told Toby that it's not polite to bite people, at which point he responded, "Yes, Mommy."

There was an article from one of the earlier issues of *The Child Psychology Magazine* called "The Biting Truth" and it said that biting is a normal part of childhood development and something that they usually outgrow before long, so I figured that was probably the case here, so I didn't think anything more of it.

CHAPTER 23

I arrived at work the next morning fifteen minutes early, which was something I liked to do and something that made my bosses happy, but it was also something that had become less frequent in recent months because I had a four-year-old son who sometimes took seven minutes to put on his socks or do any other number of simple tasks that most adults could do in seconds. I would sometimes feel embarrassed for Toby because it would take him so long to complete these simple tasks, only then I figured most other four-year-olds probably had the same difficulty, and maybe some of them took even longer.

I'd stepped out of my vehicle and started walking toward my office when I noticed an old pickup truck with a confederate flag on it, and I thought how much of a co-incidence it was to see another pickup truck with a confederate flag on it, because Timmy's father had the same type of vehicle. Only then I saw Timmy's father walking aggressively toward me, and I concluded in that moment that it must not have been a coincidence at all, and then I couldn't help but feel embarrassed for not making the connection immediately, and about how I'd just been judging Toby's intellect moments earlier, and I thought about how often it is that life teaches you lessons just at the right moments.

"I told you that you and I were going to have a fucking problem," he said, and although my company liked to describe any difficult situation as merely an opportunity, I couldn't help but conclude that his characterization was probably more accurate.

"You are upset about the biting incident," I said.

"You bet your ass."

I found it curious that Timmy's father didn't think much of the children fighting when it was his own son who was doing the bullying, even suggesting that school interference might have a tangible effect on our children's sexual orientation, only now that it was Timmy who was being bullied, he had adopted a much more protective position on the issue. Not only was this hypocritical, but it was made even more so by the fact that he was now attempting to gain my compliance in precisely the same manner that he was currently objecting to.

"How did you know where I worked?" I asked.

The question seemed to confuse him.

"What the fuck does it matter?"

The fact was that I was just curious, but I decided not to answer because he didn't seem genuinely interested in why I thought it mattered, and his nostrils were flaring out in such a way that I felt concerned for my well-being. On the last occasion Donna and the principal were present, and this may have gone a long way toward forestalling a physical confrontation.

"They are only four years old," I said.

"So what?"

"It once took Toby seven minutes to put on his socks." I said it because it was true. "And sometimes he will even defecate in his clothing." The fact is that he hadn't done so for several months now, so I hoped that it was all behind him. Then I thought that maybe it was unfair of me to disparage him this way, because he was young, and it was obviously something he couldn't help, unless maybe he was just being lazy.

Timmy's father was just looking at me funny, so I decided to continue.

"I have told Toby many things, many of which he doesn't follow or forgets moments later."

This appeared to resonate with Timmy's father, because his nostrils went back to normal, and I couldn't help thinking that perhaps the company was right after all, and that even the most difficult moments could become valuable opportunities. In this case, there was the opportunity that a tense and potentially violent episode with a bully could end up in understanding and an unlikely friendship. Only before I could consider the matter any further, he grabbed my shirt just below my throat, and it became apparent that this wasn't so much an opportunity for friendship and understanding as much as it was an opportunity that I might sustain significant personal injury.

I also couldn't help thinking about how the last person who'd grabbed me in this manner was now dismembered in a landfill. Somehow this helped keep my thoughts calm, and where I'd usually have started into some of my scary thoughts by now, and might have already reached into my trousers to fish out my Swiss army knife with the polar bear handle, possibly plunging the corkscrew into his neck or one of his eyes, instead I tried my best to remain calm and reason with him.

"There are many witnesses if you intend to assault me."

"Scared, eh?"

"No," I said, and his nostrils went back to flaring out like they had before.

"Think you're better than me, don't you?"

"No," I said, though in truth I actually did think that.

That's when I noticed one of my co-workers walking up the sidewalk.

"I believe that someone may call the police."

"You'd like that, wouldn't you?"

"No," I said.

He laughed when I said it, only then I advised him that the reason I wouldn't much like the police involved was because I was currently being investigated in relation to a missing person, and that it made things uncomfortable for me, particularly given how I was previously investigated for the murders of my landlord and a man named Sherman Dempsey.

Timmy's father didn't say anything in response, he just released me and I saw his face go white, and I think maybe he even looked a little scared. Then he looked at me with a little smile, as if he was thinking I'd smile back or laugh or otherwise indicate that I was joking, only I didn't because I wasn't.

He didn't say anything else. Instead, he just took a few steps backward and then turned around and walked back to his truck with the confederate flag bumper sticker and quickly drove away. And while the encounter hadn't resolved itself as I'd hoped it might, which might have included a handshake and the beginnings of a bond of acceptance, it at least had resolved without necessitating another drive to the local landfill.

I went upstairs to find Gordon already seated at his desk. He must have somehow noticed my disheveled look because he said "What the hell happened to you?" so I took the opportunity to tell him about the incident that had just happened downstairs, only I left off the part at the end about how many times I'd been a person of interest to the police. Gordon had actually heard some of this from the detective, but he'd been good enough not to mention it, so I figured there was no point bringing it up again. By then, I also regretted mentioning it to Timmy's father because there was no telling who he might tell, and I figured that this sort of murder gossip could make things uncomfortable at parent-teacher meetings.

"Dude got that worked up over four-year-olds?" said Gordon.

"Yes," I said.

Gordon just shook his head. "Helicopter parents," he said.

"Yes," I said.

"Blackhawk fucking Down," he added.

I didn't bother asking Gordon if he'd read last month's issue of *The Child Psychology Magazine* because to me it didn't much matter. The fact was that it had been a long time since I'd had a good friend who wasn't a dog, let alone a best friend who wasn't.

CHAPTER 24

Two weeks later Hayley was arrested.

I saw it on the local news after dinner, and they even had a short clip of her being led into the police car in handcuffs, and you could see the Morrison boy in the background wearing his cape and his helmet, and he seemed to be pretend shooting the police with a stick, only the police clearly didn't perceive him as a threat as they paid him no mind.

At first, I wasn't sure what to make of it all because I knew that Hayley was factually innocent of the crime, so I briefly thought that perhaps Hayley had committed a wholly different and completely unrelated crime, like insurance fraud or drug trafficking or maybe even prostitution, because she was fairly attractive, not that prostitutes had to be. Only then the news reporter said that she was arrested on suspicion of murder, and I reasoned that it would be too great of a coincidence for her to have committed a completely different murder, so I resigned myself to the fact that she must have just been arrested for my murder.

I'd found that people in suburbia liked to gossip, and it wasn't long before bits and pieces of information started to leak around the neighborhood. One of the neighbors even had a friend on the police force, and we learned that the search warrant had yielded some small shards of glass on the kitchen floor and fresh drops of blood that had been examined and deemed to be from Josh. This, in conjunction with the statement that I had given the detective about the fight, had apparently given them grounds for arrest.

I went to work the next day just as usual but went home early because I was feeling queasy about it and couldn't concentrate. When I told the office manager, she smiled wide and said, "I hope you feel better," but she said it in such a way as if she didn't completely believe me.

I couldn't much blame her for being suspicious though, as in my experience most people who called in sick weren't sick at all but just didn't feel like going to work that day. I knew this was the case because that same person would come into work the next day acting and behaving perfectly normal, rather than hunched over or hobbling or languishing in some other discomfort. It also happened to be that most of these people would call in sick on a Friday or Monday of a long weekend, when the rest of the weekend they were out surfing or hiking or doing any number of things that sick people usually didn't do. I felt that the office manager might view my request differently, since this was a Tuesday, and I'd already made it nearly to lunchtime, and while the look on her face and the tone of her voice suggested she might have trusted me a little, it was clear that she still didn't trust me all the way.

After saying goodbye to Gordon, I went to my car and drove home. As I stepped out of the car, I paused and looked over at Hayley's home, and I thought about Mister Muggles and wondered who was looking after him, and I wondered if maybe he'd end up living out on the streets just like the author who'd written the books that had given him his name. And I thought how that might make for an interesting story, and how maybe he would be found cold and lonely and afraid by another homeless artist, who might then also write a bestselling novel and rename Mister Muggles after one of the characters from his or her own book, and I thought how all of that would make for such a stunning and implausible coincidence. That's when I noticed a car pulling into Hayley's driveway.

"Hello there," said a woman, as she got out of her vehicle.

"Hello," I said. I hadn't seen her before, but she

looked similar to Hayley in many ways, only older. Then she introduced herself as Hayley's mother, which made a lot of sense.

"I'm sorry to hear that Hayley has been arrested," I said. I said it because it was true.

"It's absolutely not true," said the mother, and at first, I was taken aback because I wondered if she could somehow read my thoughts or had some other uncanny power of perception, only then I just as quickly realized that she was just commenting on the accusations against her daughter. "Hayley wouldn't harm a fly," she added.

"No," I said.

I felt this to be one of those casual lies that people told others, as in my experience women held not only an irrational fear, but possibly even a great animus toward all types of bugs and insects, and they not only harmed them, but did so in a very grievous and permanent way whenever possible. And though I didn't much like being lied to, I figured this was mostly just a figure of speech, so I wasn't too fussed about it, particularly given the circumstances.

"Will she be released from custody?" I asked.

"We're working on bail," she said. She seemed angry when she said it.

"Hayley is innocent," I said.

"Of course she is."

"I know that she didn't do it," I added.

She looked at me quizzically, even suspiciously, after I said it, and I thought that perhaps I shouldn't have said it quite that way, so I quickly added, "I heard that someone saw him near the horse paddock."

Her mother nodded, adding, "We've been trying to locate his best friend. Nobody has been able to find him. For all we know, they went off camping together."

His best friend was apparently someone named Doug, and from the way Hayley's mother spoke of them, she didn't think much of Josh or his friend. Only now they were apparently pinning their hopes on Doug surfacing and providing some type of alibi or innocent explanation that might assist Hayley.

"If I could just get my hands on the person who did this," she said, "I'd be the one going to jail."

From the way that she said it, I believed that she was being truthful.

"Please tell Hayley that we are thinking of her," I said.

Her mother nodded, but didn't say anything further. Instead, she turned and started walking toward Hayley's front door, but she didn't turn away in time before I saw her start to cry, and I couldn't help but think about how I was responsible for all of the pain that the family was now going through, even if Josh was a bad person and I'd acted mostly in self-defense.

I finally went inside the house, but not before stopping at the mailbox. The October issue of *The Child Psychology Magazine* had come in the mail, and although I wasn't much in the mood for reading, I decided that it might provide a pleasant distraction, so I let Molly out into the backyard and sat outside reading the latest issue.

There was an article in the new issue called "Honesty is the Best Policy" and it was all about how parents shouldn't sugarcoat difficult concepts such as divorce and death, and that it is far better to explain these things in simple yet straightforward language whenever possible; otherwise, the false or misleading information could confuse the child, and when they ultimately did learn the truth, it might even foster resentment. The article said the same thing about using the correct language for human anatomy, and while some parents felt it was better to use the words foo foo or pee pee instead of vagina or penis, the author said that you weren't so much teaching your children discretion or subtlety so much as you were teaching them to become idiots.

The article resonated with me in that moment because I couldn't help but feel how I'd inadvertently contributed to Hayley's present situation, and while I hadn't actually misled the police in any meaningful way or stated anything inaccurately, the fact was that I alone possessed information that could exonerate her from her present circumstances. This was what they called a moral dilemma, and while my parents and counselors and teachers had always told me that you can never go wrong doing the right thing, I couldn't imagine that they'd ever considered a situation where telling the truth could lead to life imprisonment, or perhaps even becoming red and open at the hands of the state. It's possible that some of these same people might have concluded that honesty wasn't necessarily the best policy in that situation as much as changing your identity or fleeing the country or perhaps some other extreme remedy that I hadn't even thought of.

I spent the rest of the day considering different alternatives to the situation that might liberate Hayley while also safeguarding myself from prosecution, only none of them seemed plausible, so by the time Donna had come home with Toby, I had resigned myself to the fact that the only way to proceed was to go to the police and confess to what I had done.

I'd briefly considered discussing the matter with Donna or Gordon, only then I figured that no good could come from that because then they would be involved, and they might even be considered accomplices or co-conspirators, and if I were to turn myself in for what I'd done it would be better to just go to the police station and do it, and so that is what I decided I needed to do.

❧❧❧

That night, I tucked Toby into bed and put Ralph under his arm. Then I took a good long look at him, and he did the same back in my direction.

"Daddy?"

"Yes?"

"Will you read me a story?"

"I do not believe that I can do justice to the voices," I said.

I thought we'd fostered an understanding by that point, but it was clear that Toby had still not given up on the matter.

"Please?"

He said it in that long, drawn-out manner that children liked to do, and while I normally had the willpower to fend him off, on this night I finally made an exception.

I asked him what story he would like to hear and he said "Tilly the Pterodactyl." I hadn't seen this one before, so I figured that Donna must have picked it up for him recently, or else perhaps he ordered it from *Scholastic Magazine* or the Bookmobile, but whichever the case, I read it aloud to him, and we looked at the pictures. The book was about a pterodactyl with anxiety who would get nervous sometimes and need to go have a look out the window to get some fresh air and a fresh perspective. Why a dinosaur was wearing shorts or living inside a house to begin with was utter nonsense, but children seemed to enjoy such plot contrivances and were seemingly more inclined to look past the fact that they were generally preposterous and filled with plot holes. I read Toby the story, and I even managed to make the closest thing I could envision to a pterodactyl noise, and even if it wasn't all the way to being a good pterodactyl, I could

tell that it was at least sufficiently good based on the
smile on Toby's face.

I couldn't help but wonder if this would be both the
first and the last time I read Toby a story, and how maybe
the next time I saw him he'd be all grown up, and that
maybe he'd even be the one to pick me up from the peni-
tentiary and have a muscle car and long hair and he might
even have some tattoos, and one of the tattoos might even
say "Dad", and I tried to imagine what his life might be
like twenty years into the future, and while I conjured up
a great many scenarios, the only thing I knew for sure
was that he'd be twenty-four years old and that to him I
would be very much a stranger. It made me sad to think it
as I kissed him on the forehead and turned off the light,
and I told him that I loved him, and he said, "I love you,
Daddy" in return, which was just about the best thing he
could have said in that moment.

I went and got ready for bed and thought that perhaps Donna might help me to achieve it one last time before turning myself into the police, only she told me that
she didn't feel like it.

Donna had been acting peculiarly toward me since
the night we'd returned from the art gala, and even
though I'd found women often acted peculiarly in one
way or another, this somehow seemed different. I thought
about simply asking her about it, but since this would
likely be our last night together, I didn't want to risk any-

thing particularly dramatic, so instead I just told her that I loved her and then we both went to sleep.

CHAPTER 25

I went to the police station first thing in the morning, only not before taking Molly for an extra-long walk and giving her peanut butter and some extra scratches behind her ears, which she always seemed to appreciate. I believe I was most sad about leaving Molly because you could explain to people why you were gone, even four-year-old people, but this was an impossible conversation to have with cats and dogs who barely knew their own names.

My car was nearly out of gas as I arrived at the police station, and though I briefly considered stopping to fill up the tank, I figured that was unnecessary at this point, under the circumstances.

There was a middle-aged lady sitting behind the

counter behind a glass partition with just a small gap at the bottom to talk.

"May I help you, sir?"

"Yes," I said.

She looked at me as if she was waiting for me to say more.

"I have come to see the detective," I said.

"The detective?" she repeated, smiling.

"Yes."

"And which one would you like? We have at least a dozen working out of this detachment."

I told her that I was here to see the English detective, and she seemed to know who I meant right away because she smiled and nodded and picked up her telephone receiver, all in that order. Then she reached for her keypad, stopping to look up at the last moment.

"Could I have your name, sir?"

I provided it easily.

"And what may I say you are calling about?"

I thought about what to say, but only for a moment.

"You may tell him that I've come to make a confession."

At the word confession, her face turned very serious, and I saw her scratch something into the notepad in front of her. Then she pressed a few buttons into her keypad and spoke very quietly into her receiver.

"If you just have a seat, he'll be with you in a moment."

I walked to the seating area where there was a woman and a child seated sleepily in two of the chairs. I could see that one of her eyes was bruised, and it was clear that both she and the child had been crying. The child wasn't much older than Toby.

"Hello," I said to the boy, only he didn't say anything back.

The woman was seated one chair beyond the boy. She looked over and gave me a weak smile then nodded.

I wasn't sure why I wanted to talk to them, all I know is that I did.

"You will be okay now. You are at the police station."

"I suppose," she said.

"This was done by the boy's father?" I said.

She got a look on her face as if I'd just said something I shouldn't, and she opened her mouth with the same expression, only then she closed it just as quickly and her demeanor softened, and instead of saying anything, she just nodded her head, and tears started streaming down her face.

"Your husband?" I asked.

She brought her hands up to her face and wiped back the tears, and finally she said, "My boyfriend," and then she brought her hand back up to wipe away some more.

"It is not right for a man to hit a woman," I said. I said it because it was true.

She got very quiet when I said this, and that's when I

first noticed the bruise on the boy's arm. He was wearing a T-shirt, and though I couldn't see the whole bruise, I could see enough of it to know that it was there.

"What is your boy's name?"

She said that his name was "Jordan," so I leaned in a bit closer and told him my name, and I asked if he would like a present for being such a brave boy for his mother. He was quiet and didn't say much, but he did nod, so I reached into my pocket and fished out my Swiss Army knife and then placed it into his hand.

"That's a polar bear on the handle," I said.

I watched his eyes light up, and he smiled for the first time. Then his mother smiled too as she wiped away more tears, only this time I think they might have been smiling tears.

"What do you say?" she said.

He said "Thank you," very softly, and I watched as he turned it over in his hand. I couldn't say precisely why I'd given it to him or why I'd even brought it with me in the first place given that I was going to the police station to confess to murder, only there was something about it that made me feel better to have it, and so I usually kept it in my pocket.

"You will need to be careful with it. I keep it sharp. It's good for whittling sticks and making spears. It is probably good for many other things, as well."

I left off the part where I had used it to kill a man named Sherman Dempsey because there was no point in sharing that information, and it probably wasn't something a young boy would want to hear.

Just then a police officer arrived and advised me that she would take me to see the detective. I got to my feet and said goodbye to the boy and his mother, then followed the police officer back into the police station. I fully expected her to deposit me into an interview room with a hot lamp and a phone book where they might extract the confession fully and freely, only instead she brought me right to the detective's office.

"Gawd blimey, now how about that, there's Sonny Jim come to visit. That's Sonny Jim, that's who we've got here."

Although this wasn't actually my name, by then I had grown accustomed to him calling me that, so I just responded as if it were.

"Pull up a chair, mate."

I took a seat in one of the two chairs in front of his desk, then he took his own seat and stared back at me from behind it.

I saw him holding onto a small piece of paper that was folded in half, and I could only assume that this was what the woman at the front desk had hastily scribbled down.

"Quite a surprise to see you today, mate. Quite a surprise indeed."

"Yes," I said.

"Don't ever be surprised by life, though, that's what

the missus always says. And she's right, you know. You just never can tell what life will offer up day to day, or even hour to hour, ain't that right, Sonny Jim?"

"No," I said.

"No," he continued, "you can never tell, can you?" He continued to hold the piece of paper in his hand.

"You'd imagine my surprise when I get a call on the blower here," he placed his free hand on top of his telephone for emphasis, "and she said a man had come to see me. And that man turned out to be my good friend Sonny Jim. And what do you say to that, mate? There's a good mate. There's a good Sonny Jim." He was smiling the whole time he was talking.

"I could see that being a surprise," I said.

"A surprise don't even cover it, mate." Then he leaned back in his chair, still cradling the paper in his hand. "And the note to boot. Gawd blimey, couldn't say I expected this one, mate. But your timing, it couldn't have been better. Couldn't have been better if you'd tried, Sonny Jim."

"I suppose."

"Bet you thought you might get a bunch of fives, eh, Sonny Jim? Couldn't be further from the truth, mate. I feel like I might even lean right over and kiss you. What make you of that, Sonny Jim?"

"I would prefer if you didn't," I said.

"Right you are. Right you are, mate." He was laughing as he said it.

The detective seemed more elated than usual. He was speaking quickly and had a large smile on his face, and he even seemed relieved.

"Well then," he said, "here I am talking nineteen to the dozen, eh, mate? Missus always says I do go on, never let the other side have a speak. That's what she tells me, that I talk too much, isn't that right, mate? There's a good mate."

I didn't much mind that he talked a lot because it kept me from saying what I had come there to say, only I knew that I still had to, knowing that Hayley was locked up in a cell somewhere in the building.

"Well then, mate," and he placed the note down on the center of his desk and tapped it twice with his finger, "shall we get on to it then?"

"Yes," I said.

"Well then, have at it," he said.

"I wish to make a confession," I said, after a moment.

"So, a confession, is it? And what a jolly good thing it is, to unburden one's soul. And that's what you're going to do today, aren't you, mate? There's a good mate if I ever saw one."

He then took out some type of recording device and turned it on, then he turned unusually silent, as if he were determined not to speak again until I did. Only by then, I'd started to have second thoughts about what I was doing, and I started thinking about the small cell that I would be locked in from that moment forward, and could feel my collar tightening around my neck. I opened my mouth to speak but didn't actually say anything. Then I looked up at the detective and saw that his smile was mostly gone and replaced by a serious look, and I could feel my nerve slipping away from me by the second, and finally, before I completely lost it, I blurted out the words as best I could.

"It was I who killed Hayley's boyfriend and dumped him in a landfill."

He just stared back at me from across the table.

"I killed him in mostly self-defense," I added.

Again, we just stared at each other, and I saw him drumming his fingers on his desk as if impatiently. Then I watched as he leaned over and scratched a few words down on a notepad, and then he placed his pen down on his desk and returned his eyes to mine.

I hadn't actually confessed, but had merely practiced the words in my mind, because I wanted to ensure that I said them exactly the right way because this was all so very important.

I was preparing to say them in the real world when I felt a lump in my throat, and I was thinking of Toby and Molly and Donna and how I might never see any of them again, and I couldn't help feeling as if I was perhaps being overwhelmed by the anxiety of the moment. Then I tried to think back to *The Child Psychology Magazine* for any tips that I might apply to my current situation, only nothing came to mind. That's when I noticed the window, and it made me think about Toby's pterodactyl book, so I decided to get up and have a look out the window to get some fresh air and a fresh perspective, and so that is what I did.

"Ho now, need a break, do you, chap? That's all right. Take a butcher's, mate. There's a good mate taking a butcher's."

I walked over to the window, and even though it was closed, it felt cooler standing beside it. I looked outside where it seemed cold and gray, and I could see the trees swaying softly in the wind. Then I heard the detective behind me.

"Not too many mates face up to the porridge. That's what I always tell the missus, bout mates not facing up to the porridge."

I tried to control my breathing in the same way that I would do when I had feelings to make people red and open, and as I slowed everything down, I started thinking about everything I had said and done to come to that moment in time, and it seemed like such a strange set of factors that had conspired to place me in that position. Finally, I started to feel more relaxed, and I was ready to return to my seat to get on with it when I suddenly saw Hayley leaving the police station all by herself, and standing as if she was waiting for someone to pick her up. I kept watching, and about a minute later someone did indeed come to collect her. I watched as a vehicle pulled up and her mother got out as well as the person I presumed was her father, and they each gave her a big hug before all three of them got back into the car and within moments they had driven away.

"Hey now, Sonny Jim, what say you?"

After another moment by the window, I stepped back over to his desk and sat down.

"So, back to it then?"

"Yes," I said.

"Well then, I'm ready to hear it, mate."

It occurred to me in that moment that it might have been a mistake attending the police station, and it made me think that perhaps the whole thing was a setup, and that perhaps Hayley had been arrested as a ploy to appeal to my conscience, assuming I had one, and I thought about how maybe she was even in on it the whole time, and how perhaps the whole thing had been an elaborate ruse.

Then I looked down at the note on his desk, and I thought I might be able to snatch it away really fast and swallow it or set it on fire or do any other number of things to dispose of the evidence, only then I remembered that I'd already told the detective that I was there to confess, and the lady at the counter as well, so I figured snatching the paper away wouldn't make much difference, and it would likely just make me look more guilty than I already was, which was a curious thing to consider, because the fact was that I knew I was already all the way guilty. "I wish to make a confession," I said, just as I'd said before.

"There's a good mate. There's a good honest mate if I ever saw one. That's what I said to myself when I first met you, that there's an honest mate if there ever was one."

I thought hard about what to say next, and while I did, I looked around the office. It wasn't much of an office. It was sparsely decorated and there was an umbrella on the floor despite the fact that there was a spot for it on the coatrack, and the only plant he had was a cactus.

"Taking a good look about you then, eh, mate? There's a good curious mate."

The detective was in good spirits, but his patience also seemed to be waning.

"I was not completely forthcoming with you when we spoke," I said.

"Figured as much. There's a man that's got more to say, that's what I told me mates here, and that's just the crux of it isn't it mate, that you've got more to say?"

"Yes."

"And it relates to the dead fellow then?"

I almost said "Yes," only then remembered that Josh was just a missing person at this point and that this was just the detective's way of trying to trick me, and while I was impressed by the clever tactic and even wanted to tell him as much, I felt it was best to not get into it, so instead I just said, "It has to do with Hayley's boyfriend."

The detective waited for me to say more, and eventually I did, after looking again at the cactus.

"The flowers," I said.

The detective got a puzzled look on his face.

"The flowers, mate?"

"Yes."

"What on earth are you talking about?"

"When you came over to visit me, and you saw the flowers on the counter. I did not actually purchase those flowers."

"The flowers?" repeated the detective.

"Yes, they were flowers for Hayley. Josh had brought them over but apparently Hayley wouldn't open the door to let him in. So I spoke to Josh briefly out in front of my house and then he gave me the flowers because he said he didn't want them."

"You sure about that, mate?"

"Not entirely," I said. "I suppose it's possible that he said he didn't need them, rather than he didn't want them."

I watched as the detective's face bent into an angry look even though he still kept the smile.

"I had taken credit for the flowers unfairly," I added.

"This was your confession, mate?"

"Yes," I said.

"Bloody hell it was. Bloody hell you came to discuss flowers," he said, and I could tell by his voice that he was growing angrier with each passing second.

"It only occurred to me after," I said, "that perhaps the flowers could have been useful in some manner."

"Is that what you thought, mate?"

"Yes."

"And how did you figure that mate, that the flowers might be useful?"

"I don't know because I am not a police officer. But perhaps they might have held his DNA, or offered some other clue to his whereabouts?"

"DNA on the flowers?" he said.

"Yes."

"A clue in the flowers?" he said

"I felt that I should tell you," I said, after a moment.

That's when he opened up the note on his desk and slammed it down in front of me.

"You've come to confess, have you, Sonny Jim, to having taken a bouquet of flowers from the man, is that what you mean to say?"

"Yes," I said.

"Anything else to confess then, mate? Maybe snuck a cookie before dinner?"

"No," I said.

"No? Then maybe you'd like to confess to having stepped on a crack in the sidewalk then, maybe to get that off your chest?"

I could tell that the detective was mocking me.

"Maybe snatched up the Lindbergh baby, eh, mate?

That's it, ain't it? There's a good mate, snatching up babies."

"No," I said.

I could tell that he was furious by then, and even if there had been previously some small room for doubt, I was now all but certain that he no longer felt that I was a good mate, not only because he was accusing me of crimes from before I was born that had already been solved, but also by the way the sweat had suddenly collected on his brow like some of the other times we'd met.

I couldn't much blame him for being angry. The fact was that I was lying to him, and he surely knew that I was lying to him, but then there wasn't much if anything at all that he could do about it. And while I didn't much like lying to the authorities, I felt that I didn't have another option in the circumstances, and while it might not have happened exactly the way I said it, the fact is that the flowers had come from Josh, so even if I was lying, I took comfort in the fact that I wasn't all the way lying.

He quickly stood up from his chair, and this time it was his turn to go over to the window, and I wondered if maybe he'd read his own son or daughter the same book that I'd read to Toby. Then I saw him look out the right side of the window where I'd seen Hayley, and he paused as he did, holding on that spot. Finally, he curled slowly back in my direction, and had the smile back on his face.

"Have a good butcher's out the window did you, Sonny Jim?"

"Yes," I said, because by then I think I finally knew what the word meant.

"Get a real good look then, did you?" he said.

"Yes," I said.

"There's a good mate, looking out windows."

He was still smiling when he said it, but it didn't seem like a happy smile because his teeth were clenched tightly together, and it certainly didn't seem as if he wanted to kiss me anymore so much as it seemed like he wanted to make me red and open. He stared at me that way a while longer and then finally invited me to leave his office, only it wasn't so much an invitation as it was an order, and he didn't use precisely those words but certain words that I don't much like repeating.

I went outside and got in my car and couldn't help but reflect on the unexpected state of my liberty. Then I took a few minutes to just stare up into the sky, and then I started thinking about outer space, and I couldn't help but wonder how far it goes and if there's an end somewhere or if it's similar to my thoughts in that it goes on and on forever and never ends, except maybe when I go to sleep.

I thought about all this until I started up my car and saw the gas light on my dashboard, so I pulled out of the police station and started driving toward the nearest gas station.

CHAPTER 26

Somehow, after all of that, I was only twenty minutes late for work, and though I half expected Mr. Peters to come by and say something to me, as luck would have it, he never did.

"You feeling better today?" asked Gordon.

"Yes," I said.

"Good. It wasn't the same without you here yester-day."

It had been a long time since anyone said something like that to me. In fact, I couldn't help but think that some people were more comfortable when I wasn't around than when I was. Not just by the way they acted toward me, but by the fact that sometimes they even told me so.

"I will try not to go away again," I said. "Though it

is possible I could become sick or injured in some fashion, and in that case, it may happen again. Or if I go on vacation with Donna and Toby, as we are sure to do at least three weeks in the year."

Gordon just stared at me when I said it. He was wearing his sunglasses inside again, and even though I couldn't see his eyes, it was clear that I'd said something that perplexed him.

"You really are a fucking weirdo, aren't you?" he said.

I had been called that word and many others over the years, but unlike hearing it from Josh or Timmy's father or my former landlord, it didn't seem as if Gordon said it to hurt me.

"Well, you go on being weird," he said, turning back to his special keyboard. "Enough phonies in this world already."

"Yes, there are," I said.

I said it because it was true.

ↁↈↁ

As I drove home, I couldn't help but think back on my good fortune that day. I had come very close to confessing to the murder of Hayley's boyfriend, and while I suppose there was always the possibility that the detective would have thanked me for coming clean and patted me on the back, and we could have sat around and had a good chat about it, I believe the much more likely scenario would have seen me immediately wrestled to the floor and beaten into submission and then clapped into irons, and how I'd probably already be wearing a prison jumpsuit, presuming they had one in my size.

I arrived to find that Donna was already home making dinner, while Toby was playing in the other room with some Lego while Molly slept quietly by his side, and it seemed very much like the happy ending that you always read about in Toby's stories. Of course, there was always the possibility that the detective's investigation would continue, and that one day they might exhume enough pieces of Josh from the landfill to expose my murder, and that maybe I would be clapped into irons after all, and sent to while away the rest of my days in a small cold cell, or perhaps even be subjected to a lifetime of hard labor—if that was something they still did.

But instead of all that, I had a normal family dinner, and then did normal family things, such as eating dessert and watching television. Donna was acting relatively normal that day, so I felt that perhaps she would help me to achieve it before we went to sleep, so as Donna got Toby ready for bed, I took Molly for a long walk around the neighborhood. We were just coming back around the block when I saw Hayley stepping down her front steps with Mister Muggles. I couldn't help but wonder if Hayley had been part of a ruse with the detective, so although I still approached her, I did so with caution.

"Hello," I said, once I was sufficiently satisfied that she'd seen me.

"Hi," she said.

"I see that you have secured your release from custody," I said.

She nodded, but didn't say anything.

"All accused persons have a right to reasonable bail," I said. I had not only learned this from my law class, but had done some research on the issue in the past in the event that I found myself incarcerated for any of my own crimes.

"Thanks," she said, "but nobody bailed me out. They dropped the charges."

"I see."

"Worst twenty-four hours of my life," she said, and her voice began to buckle.

I could see that the topic upset her, so I tried to change it.

"I met your mother," I said. "She seemed very nice."

"Yeah, she is," said Hayley, only she didn't seem very interested in changing the subject, because then she went right back into it. "Thing is, they wouldn't tell me why they let me go. Just that 'new information's come to light' or something like that."

"It is possible they wish to keep the information secret in the event it compromises an ongoing investigation."

"Yeah, they mentioned something along those lines,

too. Only thing is, I found out anyway. Why they let me go, that is."

Molly and Mister Muggles were sniffing around each other and biting and growling, but it was just friendly bites and growls between dogs, so neither of us interrupted them.

"It was Josh's friend. He called me today. Just got back from some fishing trip in Ontario or something."

I figured that she was referring to Doug, whom her mother had mentioned when I met her, and soon enough I didn't need to figure at all because she started to say his name.

"Doug had a bunch of messages from me and Josh's mother and even the police, so he called the police and apparently told them all about the last time he'd talked to Josh. Turns out Josh had called Doug and told him all about our fight. About how he broke his hand smashing a glass. All of it."

As it turned out, Hayley hadn't been part of any ruse to get me to confess, but had herself become the chief suspect until Doug's statement had not only provided an innocent explanation for Josh's blood in the kitchen, but had also proven him to be safely out of Hayley's home in the hours after the fight. And I couldn't help thinking about how funny it was the way things worked in life, and that had Doug left one night earlier for his fishing trip, he never would have been available for Josh to call, which means he never would have been able to exonerate

Hayley. And then on the other side, if Doug hadn't come back precisely when he did, then Hayley would never have been released from custody when she was, so I wouldn't have seen her out the window at that exact moment, and how then I likely would have confessed to the crime and been clapped into irons after all, and set to while away the rest of my days in a small cold cell, or perhaps even subjected to a lifetime of hard labor—if that was something they still did.

Hayley looked around and said, "I don't know how I'm going to show my face around here anymore."

"The police have cleared you of any wrongdoing," I said.

"You think that matters around here?"

"I know that you didn't kill him," I said.

"How do you know?" and then I saw a funny look on her face, and I couldn't help but think that maybe I'd said too much.

"A man said he saw him at the horse paddock," I said.

"Mmm."

"And his friend said he was in good health," I added.

"I suppose," she said, then added, before long, "but then what the hell happened to him?"

"The world is a big place," I said. "He could be anywhere."

Much like asking customers if they'd like us to check the stock of certain vacuums, even though we knew we had hundreds, I felt that if Hayley wished to extrapolate my comments into believing that Josh was still alive somewhere, instead of deposited in a landfill, then that was her own business. And of course, he was somewhere in the world, so it wasn't a complete lie, even if the somewhere was a landfill, and he was dismembered at my hands in mostly self-defense.

"He wasn't so bad, you know?" She said it in a sad, longing way that made me sad to hear it.

What I knew and Hayley knew and probably her mother and maybe even Mister Muggles if he truly was as smart as a pig, or just a shade below, was that Josh was going to continue to hurt her, especially when he was drinking, and while I knew that didn't justify what I'd done, I at least felt that my actions had likely saved Hayley from ongoing physical and psychological abuse.

I'd read in "Bullying Is The New Purple" that kids often learned bullying behavior from their parents, and that not only included themselves being bullied, but it often included watching their mothers being bullied by their fathers. And the article talked about how abused women rarely left bad relationships because they were stuck in what the author called "a cycle of violence," which meant they were too scared to leave or maybe had low self-esteem, or a host of other reasons. And I could tell by the way Hayley was speaking right now that there was a real possibility that she would have forgiven him and taken him back, and then the cycle of violence would have repeated itself, so while I remained remorseful about what I'd done, I couldn't say that I was all the way remorseful.

I never did respond to her comment because the fact was that I felt that he was indeed a bad person, and I figured I'd already lied to her and misled her enough. So instead, I just petted Mister Muggles and told him that he was a good boy, which he certainly was. Then I said goodnight to Hayley, only just before I was able to leave, she reached forward and gave me a long hug and even kissed me softly on my cheek, and while I felt somewhat uncomfortable accepting this affection, knowing what I had done and the pain that I'd caused her, I thought it wasn't my place to object, so I didn't.

I took Molly inside, but not before stopping to check the mailbox, and it was a good thing that I did, because I found a piece of mail addressed to me, so I placed this in my pocket to read before bed that night.

The lights were all off downstairs, so I went upstairs to check on Toby but found that he was already fast asleep because of my long walk with Molly and my chat with Hayley. Still, I crept quietly into his bedroom and gave him a kiss on his cheek before closing his door, which was something that my mother and father used to do with me, and something I very much enjoyed, so I figured that Toby probably enjoyed it too. Then I entered my own bedroom and found Donna packing a suitcase, and I figured that she must be going on a trip that I didn't know about, only when I looked closer I saw that the suitcase was mine and so were the clothes, so as it turns out the person going on a trip was me.

"What are you doing?" I asked.

She didn't answer.

"Why are you packing my things?" Still, she didn't answer, she just continued to pack my suitcase in a rather rushed and aggressive manner, not taking the due care she should, particularly with the more delicate fabrics.

It was obvious that it was no longer a question of whether Donna would help me to achieve it that night, but a question of whether I would be able to remain in the house, and whether or not we would even remain together as a couple, and while it would be easy enough for us to split up the pets, dividing Toby would be far more complicated.

"You are upset," I said.

"You're damn right I'm upset."

"I do not understand."

"I saw the marks on the back of your neck," she said.

"The marks?"

As it turned out, Donna had seen the marks on my neck and some bruising on my back after we'd returned from the rooftop gala, and she had presumed incorrectly that I was having an affair, and had further extrapolated that during the course of the sexual rendezvous that I had engaged in some type of rough sex or otherwise sado-masochistic sexual activity.

"I'd been wondering why the hell my concealer had been running so low. Never thought. Never thought in a million years..." Then she held up and it looked as if she might cry.

I thought about offering a weak explanation, but nothing immediately came to mind, and the fact was that I knew that I couldn't tell her the real reason that I was using the concealer, and so I felt that adultery was probably a better explanation than murder, all things considered, even if it wasn't a very good one. At the same time, though, I didn't want to admit to something I hadn't done, so instead I just chose silence.

"Was it Hayley?"

As it turns out, saying nothing at all wasn't any better than a weak explanation, as she had concluded from my silence that I had indeed admitted to the act.

"No," I said, although Hayley was an attractive woman, and I suppose that if I did want to achieve it with someone other than Donna, I would have been perfectly content doing so with Hayley, only I left that last part off because I couldn't imagine it would have assisted my current situation.

"Did you do it?" she said, suddenly raising her voice and slamming some of my clothes down into the suitcase. "Did you kill her fucking boyfriend?"

It was a difficult situation, because I had, in fact, killed Hayley's boyfriend, only she had arrived at that conclusion from an incorrect assumption, so I felt that it wasn't very fair of her to have discovered the truth about me by accident.

"Why would you say such a thing?" I asked, which was a way to both evade the question and not lie to her.

"I saw you two," she said, and I realized that she must have been watching from the window.

"She is upset," I said.

"Well then, why don't you go console her?"

And though it didn't seem like a genuine offer, I decided to respond that I'd already tried my best, and this seemed to be the wrong answer, since she slapped me hard across the face after I'd said it.

This was the first time that Donna had ever laid a hand on me in anger, and while at first I was shocked and perhaps even hurt, it was only a moment later that I started to think some of my scary thoughts, but just as quickly as they started, I did my best to push them away, and as Donna immediately began to cry, it became easier.

"Just go," she said, turning away and pulling her hands to her face.

"Where will I go?" I asked, only she didn't answer.

I decided not to prod any further, as it was clear she wasn't in the mood to assist me with a discussion about alternate accommodations. Instead, I just turned to finish packing my mostly packed suitcase. As it turns out, she had done a remarkable job in selecting my favorite and most commonly worn clothing, and though I wanted to mention this to her by way of offering praise, I had by then resigned myself that it was likely the less I talked the better.

I said a long goodbye to Molly and then finally got into my car and drove to a nearby hotel. When I checked in, the young clerk asked me "How many nights?" and I told him that I didn't know, and this seemed to confuse the clerk, so then I explained that Donna had wanted me to leave that night, but that she didn't specify the number of nights that she wanted it.

The clerk shrugged his shoulders when I said it, then he slid the key across the counter, so I took it and then brought my suitcase to the room.

It wasn't much of a hotel room. The drapes and the carpet were dated, and the bed was small, and the pillows weren't very comfortable, but at least it had a small television and it seemed relatively clean.

I set my things up in the bathroom as I did at home and then got ready for bed, which included brushing my teeth, and after I got in bed, I thought back on the last twelve or so hours and couldn't help but think about how strange the day had been. My company called this a paradigm shift, which meant that many things in life were just a matter of perspective, and how perspectives could often quickly change. So while things looked bad with Donna and I was sleeping in a hotel away from my family and Molly, I couldn't help but think about how fortunate I was not to be locked in a small jail cell.

One thing I did regret was not managing a better explanation to Donna, because looking back on the things I did and said I saw that they likely made me look guilty of being an adulterer, even though I was in fact innocent of this. I was thinking of all this when I suddenly remembered the letter in my pocket, and even though I was in bed and all the lights were off, my curiosity got the better of me, so I went over to where I'd laid my pants and fished out the letter from the pocket and turned on a light.

It was an unusual letter because it didn't look like any of the bills or junk mail I normally received, and I didn't recognize the return address. I opened it carefully because sometimes I liked to keep certain mail and correspondence by placing it back in the same envelope in which it had come, and even if I didn't have to use the exact same envelope that it came in, there was something about using another envelope that seemed inappropriate, so I avoided having to do that whenever I could.

The document was unusual, and while it took me some time to read it all the way through, I quickly discovered that it was a summons for jury duty.

It wasn't much of a summons. The font was too small and they'd misspelled my last name, and it was also rather demanding. It said that I had to appear for jury duty next month, and that failing to attend could result in my arrest and even a seizure of assets, which seemed quite heavy-handed for a government document.

I returned the summons to its envelope and turned the light off and got back into bed. I wasn't too fussed about the summons because I figured the likelihood of me actually being selected was slim.

Then I again thought about how badly the day had ended, with Donna being angry with me and living out of a hotel away from Molly and Toby. Only then just as quickly I started thinking about how differently this day could have ended, and how I could just as easily be in a small prison cell with an even smaller bed and even harder pillows, and so I figured that even if the ending wasn't all the way happy, it was at least sufficiently happy.

And I thought that even if I wasn't welcome home right away, I would at least see Gordon at work, and maybe even go to the ice cream shop and see the man who was probably named Steve, and I thought how maybe I'd even watch to see if his mood would change depending on what flavor of ice cream people ordered. And as I considered all of this, I thought that maybe the detective was right all along, and that maybe I was "a good curious mate," only then I got very sleepy, so I didn't think about being a good curious mate for very long.

Next

The Introvert Bears Filthy Witness

Newly estranged from Donna, the introvert will be selected as one of twelve jurors on a notorious murder trial,
forcing him to navigate uncomfortable social interactions
with numerous members of the public, this time with no
avenue of escape.

About the Author

Michael Paul Michaud is an author and lawyer in the Greater Toronto Area. An American-Canadian citizen, he holds a B.A. in English, Honors B.A. in Political Science (summa cum laude), and a J.D. in Law. He has also made regular appearances on SiriusXM Radio's "Canada Talks."

The Introvert Confounds Innocence is Michaud's third release. His chief literary influences are Orwell, Dickens, Vonnegut, and Dostoevsky.

fb.com/michaelpaulmichaud

CPSIA information can be obtained
at www.ICGtesting.com
Printed in the USA
LVHW021912040419
613047LV00007B/26

9 781644 371213